D1521438

The Old Castle in Austria

Sins of the Fathers

Mathilde Apelt Schmidt

iUniverse, Inc.
New York   Bloomington

The Old Castle in Austria

Sins of the Fathers

iUniverse books may be ordered through booksellers or by contacting:

iUniverse
1663 Liberty Drive
Bloomington, IN 47403
www.iuniverse.com
1-800-Authors (1-800-288-4677)

ISBN: 978-0-595-52491-4 (pbk)
ISBN: 978-0-595-62544-4 (ebk)

Printed in the United States of America

iUniverse rev. date: 1/9/2009

Table of Contents

Acknowledgments..vii

Introduction...ix

PROLOGUE 1975...1

BOOK ONE 1980-1986...5

    CHAPTER 1 The Castle 7

    CHAPTER 2 Viktor... 13

    CHAPTER 3 Gerda... 21

    CHAPTER 4 Betty... 29

    CHAPTER 5 Sepp 47

    CHAPTER 6 Adele... 61

BOOK TWO 1987...65

    CHAPTER 7 Brenner's Visit................................... 67

    CHAPTER 8 Vienna.. 77

    CHAPTER 9 Confession 87

    CHAPTER 10 Forgiveness 95

    CHAPTER 11 August.. 103

BOOK 3 1991..109

    CHAPTER 12 Raphael 111

    CHAPTER 13 California....................................... 117

BOOK FOUR 1995-1996 137

    CHAPTER 14 Reunion.. 139

    CHAPTER 15 Neusiedl Lake, Revenge 149

    CHAPTER 16 The Aftermath... 167

    CHAPTER 17 Reminiscence... 177

    CHAPTER 18 Closure.. 183

EPILOGUE Beyond 1996 187

List of Characters..191

Explanation of German Expressions...........................195

Acknowledgments

As I find that the most difficult part of writing is the line editing, I can't express enough gratitude to my tireless readers, my daughter Doris Schmidt Michaels, my niece Phyllis Kreider, and, above all, my daughter Barbara Schmidt Cruz. I can't thank these accomplished readers enough since my own ability to produce a "clean" manuscript is spotty at best. Having been raised and educated in Germany for thirty-two of my eighty-seven years, I still harbor "Germanisms" in my speech as well as in my writing. Not even taking several classes in English writing and grammar has been instrumental in erasing these shortcomings. However, a fervent wish to express myself in the language spoken and read by the people around me induces me to write now—one book after the other.

I also thank my grandson, Denali Schmidt, for creating the cover picture.

The helpful staff at iUniverse has patiently guided me through the various steps of publishing my books, four so far, and will do so in the future.

Thank you, all.

Mathilde Apelt Schmidt, Fall of 2008.

Introduction

While looking at photos taken on trips to Europe during my long life I came upon a snapshot of a castle on a hill in Southern Austria. This castle, originally a monastery, used to belong to relatives of my father. My husband and I had a chance to visit this castle after it had been sold and the new owner—the widowed mother of seven children, six boys and a little girl—graciously allowed us to visit and showed us around. The beauty of the place, the lovely surrounding landscape, and the picturesque views from the tall windows of the second story impressed us deeply. I could see in my mind the former owners of the castle, a poet and writer, and his second wife, who was my father's sister, and the children of his first wife—one of them the husband of my sister—living and working in these halls and rooms. The day of our visit happened to be part of a celebration in memory of the great writer and poet, the owner of the castle from 1922 to his death in 1933. People from the castle and the surrounding village were performing in his honor a play written by him in the big *Rittersaal* (hall of the warriors). I had already composed a short story about this castle in my collection of stories, *The Lake Dwellers,* peopling it with fictional characters. That story became this novel, *The Old Castle in Austria,* set in the time period of the 1970s to the 1990s.

In my book I have the descendant of the Austrian writer/owner marry an American widow and therefore the setting is not only in Austria but in California as well. Also Gypsies and an Asian are included in the list of characters. The plot develops slowly around these people and touches upon a few controversial issues. The protagonist of my story is the old castle, observing changes over the years.

Many of the old European castles have their *Spuks,* pronounced like "spooks," inexplicable haunting sounds coming from the attic, heard only by oversensitive people, and hardly ever explained. The castle that my husband and I had visited had the very imaginative owner's wife—my aunt—pick up sounds of peas falling and rolling above her head. She called them *Erbsenspuk,* and she created ghost stories surrounding those spooky sounds. Since I had read her stories and was curious about the reality of these *Spuks,* I asked the new owner if they were still detected. She laughed and insured me that the attic had been thoroughly cleaned; that some animals had made their home in all the rubbish accumulated over the years, and no; no more *Spuks.*

Prologue

1975

In the small church in Blauenwald, next to the castle of the same name, the congregation suffered in the stifling heat. It was a sultry Sunday morning in July. The young priest, Raphael Garibaldi, had given a heartfelt sermon on the topic of forgiveness. He invited his flock to confess their sins at the end of the service. He was tired and had a hard time keeping focused.

As he entered the confession booth, he invited the first penitent to confess. When he recognized the voice of Gerda Wanz, the housekeeper at the castle, he perked up. Gerda muttered in a timid voice, "O my God, I am heartily sorry; I feel deeply in love with you, my priest. Tell me what I can do."

Raphael was stunned. He did not know what to say. At last he uttered, "Go home and pray, so God might forgive you. Attend tonight's Mass and take the Holy Eucharist." Gerda rose up from the low bench where she had been kneeling, sighed from the bottom of her heart, and left the church.

The young priest had hardly recuperated from the shock when he recognized another voice, this one belonging to Viktor Baumeister, the son of his landlord, the castle owner Alfred Baumeister. "O God, I am so very sorry. I've sinned gravely. A Gypsy girl is pregnant with my child. I had been drinking with my friends and forced myself on her. She was young and inexperienced, and she trusted me. I do not love the young woman and cannot marry her. I gave her money and sent her away. I forbade her to ever return to Blauenwald. Please, Father, tell me, is there salvation for me?" Raphael was shocked almost more profoundly by this second confession. Viktor was his good friend, about the same age as he, close to thirty years old. He should have known better. Raphael knew about Viktor's drinking problem. This leaving the path of righteousness just once had led to consequences for which Viktor would have to pay dearly. He must atone for it. What could Raphael say to him?

He told him, "Go home and pray. You have done a great wrong to the young woman and also to the seed inside her. Do whatever you can to lighten her burden. God will help you. Come tonight and do penance to absolve your sins."

The young priest stepped out of the booth and looked to see if there were other penitents. No one was waiting in front of the curtain. Raphael left the now empty church.

Outside the congregation was gathered, socializing and waiting for the priest to come out and shake their hands. Raphael shook the sweaty palms of about eighty parishioners, farmers with their families, workers, business owners and, at the very end of the line, the castle owners, Alfred and Susanne Baumeister and their son, Viktor. Did he detect tenseness when taking Viktor's hand into his? Raphael pressed the hand warmly and looked deeply into Viktor's eyes. They said nothing. Confession is private.

Gerda left immediately after confession and went up to the castle entrance, mounted the granite staircase to the upper floor, and walked through the hallway to her room in the east wing. Was it fate that the priest, the object of her deep love, had his room next to hers? A little while later she heard him entering the wing, opening his door, and closing it softly. She sat down on her bed, thinking about her decision to finally confess what was in her heart. What irony! She was so close to him but would never get any closer. Raphael was an ambitious man. His goal was to become a cardinal and he had achieved the first step of the difficult ladder: Priesthood. He would not stray—not ever. Gerda got up, changed into her housekeeper's uniform—a simple black dress and a white apron—assembled her keys, and started her day's work.

Next door the priest took off his alb, changed into comfortable clothes, and sat down at his desk. He could not concentrate and contemplated what he had just heard during confession. How difficult life could be! Here he, a dedicated member of the Holy Catholic Church, was living next to this wonderful woman who loved him—him, Raphael Garibaldi, who had given his vows to the highest authority of his church, to God. To break these vows meant giving up his life's goal. He had to be steadfast and not give way to temptation.

Raphael also thought of Viktor, who had given in to carnal desire while intoxicated. Would he ever find atonement? Raphael decided to help Viktor make the right decisions. Viktor should send enough money to the young woman and make sure that the baby—his own child—would be welcome at the castle in case something should happen to the mother. Raphael had deep sympathy for the migrant Romany tribe, as the Gypsies were called in Kosovo. He knew that most Gypsies were good Catholics. He had enough influence through his status as priest to contact churches in other Baltic states and find out about the young woman and her baby.

BOOK ONE

1980-1986

CHAPTER 1

The Castle

The castle Blauenwald was situated on top of a hill in southern Styria in the beautiful geographically diversified country of Austria. It was visible from afar and had been a landmark for many centuries. The name meant "Blue Forest" and had been chosen because of the bluish needles of the spruce trees that dominated the surrounding forests.

The history of the castle was varied. Originally it had been built by the Catholic Church as a monastery to house a group of monks whose obligation was to convert the wild tribes migrating from Asia during the thirteenth century to the Christian faith. The monks lived in a one-story building consisting of four wings erected around a square courtyard. One wing housed the kitchen and dining area; the other wings were designed to be used as sleeping and working areas for the monks. Part of the north wing was a chapel for a time. The monks entered the courtyard through a gate from the north. Changes in the appearance of the castle took place during changes of Austria's history.

Austria was ruled by the ancient house of Hapsburg for seven centuries. The country became an empire after the abolition of the Holy Roman Empire in 1804 and emerged as one of the three European dominant powers after the Congress of Vienna when Napoleon was defeated at Waterloo in 1815 (together with Prussia and Russia). Emperor *Franz Josef* (Francis Joseph, also King of Hungary, 1830-1916) led the country for most of the latter half of the 1800s and until his death during World War I. During his rule the dual-monarchy *Österreich-Ungarn* (Austria-Hungary) was formed, which lasted until the end of World War I when Austria became a republic. A cousin of the emperor fell in love with the unique layout of the building. He acquired it, paying a high price that the ever-hungry monks could not resist, and renovated the original austere edifice to become a castle fit for royalty. Using the money they got from the sale, the monks found a different shelter and were able to continue their good works for a while until they gradually disbanded the order.

The castle's new owner added a second story to the structure and built a magnificent granite staircase leading from the courtyard to the second floor incorporating arcs supported by Greek columns. The royal family occupied the upper floor, and the serving staff lived downstairs. While the monks had worshipped in the chapel that was part of the north wing, the emperor's cousin erected a beautiful church with a bell tower adjoining the castle on the south side. At six o'clock every morning the bells of the church—except on Sundays—rang, and life began in Blauenwald. This practice still continued while our story took place. The owner also constructed stables and carriage houses for the numerous vehicles needed for the royal family. On top of the original chapel and above the entrance to the courtyard a large ballroom, later called *Rittersaal,* because of scenes depicting knights in armor painted on the inside walls, stretched across the entire north wing of the castle. Ceiling-to-floor windows on both elongated sides of this huge hall allowed the visitors, who climbed up the colossal stairway to the royal quarters, to enjoy the vista of lovely hills toward the city of Graz.

Around the castle, the village of Blauenwald was growing and thriving. The dense spruce forests gradually gave way to farmland. The Mediterranean climate allowed the growing of grapes, and several wineries sprang up in the area.

The castle was owned by nobility only for a short while. After the royal cousin of the emperor suffered financial difficulties toward the end of the nineteenth century, a wealthy businessman purchased the estate and kept up the premises. Blauenwald has stayed in private hands ever since. At the beginning of the twentieth century the castle belonged to a gambler who died during World War I, and his heirs neglected the premises. Nothing was done to keep up the buildings and the land.

The castle was put up for sale in this dilapidated state but nobody seemed to be interested in purchasing it. In 1922 the writer Rudolf Baumeister, a dashing, life-loving man, and his talented, artistic wife, Maria, were searching for a quiet place in the country. They had met and fallen in love while both were still locked in unfulfilled marriages. Rudolf had married Friederike von Ebersbach, a rich heiress, about eight years older than he and in poor health. They had a son, Alfred. Maria also had an older and quite wealthy husband. She had no children. Only after both spouses had passed away were Rudolf and Maria able to get married and inherit the money that made it possible for them to travel. After having lived in cramped quarters in Vienna—together with Rudolf's son Alfred and their own love child, Karl, conceived before they could marry—they enjoyed their newly found freedom.

Alfred was sent off to a boarding place in Vienna and went to school, first to a boys' *Gymnasium,* then to college. He hardly ever met with his parents. They took Karl with them on their many holiday trips.

After a while they got tired of traveling and started looking for a place to stay and to raise Karl properly. They found the Blauenwald estate desirable and affordable. They bought the castle, improved buildings and land, and enjoyed living there for many happy years. When the inheritance money ran out, they started to work again, Rudolf his writing, Maria her painting. Their land also provided for sustenance.

What most attracted the Baumeisters was the calm serenity of the estate. Eventually they restored the premises and improved the neglected buildings and the unattended fields and forests around it, using the proceeds from Rudolf's books and Maria's artwork to pay for the construction. Their happiness was impaired when Hitler's troops marched into Austria in 1938, were practically handed the country without even a gunshot, and intended to make Castle Blauenwald their headquarters. Only Maria's steadfast refusal to leave the castle prevented the Nazis from taking over their home.

Austria had become a province of Germany, and for eight long years the country did not exist as an independent state. It was referred to under the name of *Ostmark.* For about eight years the name *Österreich* did not appear in atlases, dictionaries, or any other official works. Only after the end of World War II were printers allowed again to refer to the country by its original name.

In 1939 World War II broke out and Karl Baumeister was drafted. He was a brilliant young man, taking after his grandfather, loving life, women, and wine. For him, war was a big adventure. Alfred was past drafting age and was already managing the estate for his parents. Toward the end of the war Karl was killed by friendly fire. He was only thirty years old and he did not even die as a hero in battle. The grieving parents lived on for a few years, keeping Blauenwald up with Alfred's help. The household was taken care of by a capable housekeeper and Alfred's wife, Susanne, whom he had met and married in Vienna while still studying there.

When, in the beginning of the 1950s, the older Baumeisters died one after the other, they were laid to rest in the family vault outside the castle. The entire community of Blauenwald attended the funerals.

Alfred and Susanne Baumeister were now the official owners of the estate and maintained castle and land in mint condition. With one exception: no one thought of cleaning up the attic. It had been used for storing discarded furniture and other rubbish since the beginning of the 20th Century.

Like most castles in Austria Blauenwald had its *Spuk.* According to *Frau* Margarete Schwarz, strange sounds were heard above her room from time to time. She was an expert on such indicative noises. The older Baumeisters had hired her as housekeeper when they bought the castle. She was then a young married woman from the village who moved with her husband Fritz to a little apartment on the second floor of the castle. In 1980, when our story begins, she had lived in the castle for close to fifty years and she heard rackets above her room on the upper east wing of the castle. Shuffling and bumping noises increased when the war broke out in 1939, when Karl was killed, when the old Baumeisters died, and when a drought or a flooding was threatening the harvest of the crops. For some mysterious reason it was only *Frau* Grete, as most people called her, who perceived these noises. Maybe *Frau* Grete slept more lightly or had a more vivid imagination than the others who occupied the eastern wing—in any event, some people just shrugged their shoulders, and some believed her. But no one ever went up to the attic to check what was going on up there.

Alfred and Susanne were responsible owners. Alfred had been well educated in the fields of agronomics, viniculture, and general estate management at the *Hochschule für Bodenkultur* (Academy for Agriculture) in Vienna. He used his knowledge and expertise to develop the fertile lands of Blauenwald, not only to keep up the fields of vegetables for feeding people and animals on the estate, but also to turn it into a profitable *Weingut,* raising grapes for the manufacturing of wine. He had bought most of the vines in northern Italy, where he and his wife went often on vacation. Many of the grapes were of the green variety. The Baumeisters' specialty was the Muscat vine that produced large, golden berries, resulting in the fruity Muscatel wine. Alfred and Susanne did not process their grapes—they took their harvest to Reichenfels, the neighboring village, where their good friend Manfred Sattler had presses and wine-making equipment.

The younger Baumeisters had married in 1933, the same year their countryman Adolf Hitler took over the power in neighboring Germany. Only five years later Austria would become a province of Germany and be part of Hitler's "Thousand-Year Empire," that so abruptly ceased to exist in 1945.

Over the years the old castle observed generations come and go.

CHAPTER 2

Viktor

Two years after the end of World War II, the Baumeisters had a son, Viktor. He still remembered his old grandparents—Rudolf, wearing loose cotton clothes and a wide-brimmed hat, strolling over his fields and vineyards with his dog, the German shepherd Prinz, accompanied by pleasantly plump Maria in flowing white garments, holding a parasol.

After the parents were laid to rest, Alfred and Susanne made the most needed reconstructions, improving the castle and the grounds even more, and, leaving the estate in the hands of a capable manager, took to traveling with young Viktor. During the mid 1950's they stayed home and again took over the management of the estate while Viktor went to school, first in Blauenwald, and then to high school in nearby Graz, the capital of Styria. After his graduation from high school, his parents enrolled him at the same academy in Vienna where Alfred had studied estate management. Viktor was supposed to take over the management of the castle and grounds after his graduation from the academy. Alfred and Susanne assumed that their son would settle down by the time they were ready to retire. However, unlike his father, more like his Uncle Karl, young Viktor took to dawdling and he did not apply himself to serious studying. The Baumeisters were ready to be relieved from managing the estate and yearned to resume their traveling.

When in 1970 Susanne Baumeister fell ill with the flu during an epidemic that was raging in that part of the country, she was too tired to deal with the large household. *Frau* Grete Schwarz, the capable housekeeper, who used to run the entire household, also became elderly and had to limit her realm of duties to being only the cook. Susanne remained sickly even after recovering from the flu. She needed help with the household. At the same time Josef Wanz, Sepp for short—only twenty-three at the time—was hired as manager of the Blauenwald estate. He convinced his younger sister, Gerda, born in 1949, to apply for the job of housekeeper at the castle to relieve the mistress of the task of running the large household. The Baumeisters were in good financial shape at that time and gave Gerda the job. They were satisfied with her work. With the estate in good hands and Viktor away from home, they relaxed. As soon as Susanne felt a little better, they started traveling again.

Their first longer trip was to the Amalfi Coast in Italy. They stayed in fashionable Positano for two wonderful weeks, enjoying boat trips on the open Mediterranean Sea, and touring the lovely surroundings of the "vertical" city. In the ancient city of Amalfi they met the young Catholic cleric Raphael Garibaldi, who was slightly older than their son, Viktor. He was their tour guide at the ancient cathedral, and he impressed the Baumeisters as being a young man of deep devotion to the Catholic Church, possessing intrinsic knowledge, and demonstrating a warm personality. Rail thin, of soul-stirring rhetoric, and fluent in the German language, he touched Susanne's heart. After he had told the group he was leading through the sanctuary that he was an ordained priest (amazingly young for this achievement) and was looking for a job, Susanne talked to Alfred. "Our priest in Blauenwald is getting too old. The church council has to look for a replacement. How about suggesting this young man who obviously needs a job? He seems to be very qualified. For him working in our parish would be more satisfying than guiding tourists."

Alfred also was impressed by the sincerity of the young priest and promised him to talk to their church council. They recommended him on their return to Blauenwald. Raphael applied for the position and was hired. This happened in the same year Sepp and Gerda Wanz were hired.

The designated young priest proved to do his job well. People in Blauenwald trusted him. They went to confession after Sunday mass, and soon Raphael knew more about the people in Blauenwald than anyone else. The new priest was offered a room in the east wing of the castle, next to Gerda's room.

Two confessions in 1975 stirred him deeply. The first was Gerda Wanz's declaration about her deep feelings for him, Raphael. The second was by Viktor Baumeister about his affair with the young Gypsy girl. Later he found out from talking to Viktor that her name was Adele and that she was only fourteen years old when Viktor took advantage of her. It cost him many prayers and total dedication to his church guidelines to confront both problems.

All through the 1970's the Baumeisters traveled. Most of their trips were to Mediterranean countries: Greece, Italy, and Spain. One of their favorite spots was the amazing Tuscany wine land. They had purchased their famous Muscat grapes there and frequently revisited the area. Again and again, they were fascinated by the beauty of the countryside and the efficiency of the vineyards, and they invested in more and even better Muscat vines. When they came home after their trips, they enjoyed being back in their comfortable home and surroundings. Under their guidance the premises of Blauenwald flourished.

Viktor, the only son of the castle owners, was a late bloomer, a playboy, loving good times with wine and women. He was not a bad man, just not dedicated to his future. He was spoiled. His parents had sent him to the same agricultural academy in Vienna where Alfred had gone, but instead of taking advantage of this great opportunity and buckling down, he dawdled, neglected his studies, and refused to grow up. He traveled much. People in the village around the castle did not think very highly of him. They had seen the Gypsy girl with him and had suspicions.

Alfred and Susanne had no idea about the plight their son and their housekeeper were in. Viktor was secretive about his escapades and the only knowledgeable person was the priest, Raphael. Or so he thought. Some people in Blauenwald still remembered the young Gypsy girl Adele, her friendship with Viktor, and her sudden disappearance. Rumors about this were still floating around ten years later. Sepp Wanz, who had his eyes open about what was going on with the castle owners, had heard those rumors but could not substantiate any of them. He had his own secrets to hide and did not talk much. Gerda, his sister, was involved with problems of her own and her household chores. She had neither inclination nor time to listen to gossip.

* * *

Nobody could foresee the horrible turn of events that happened in 1980 when both owners of Castle Blauenwald suddenly died in a car crash. Alfred and Susanne were traveling in Tuscany, driving on a narrow road during heavy ground fog. The winding road led to the lovely town of Siena, where they intended to visit their favorite vineyard and to buy more vines. A speeding car coming from Siena dashed around a corner and the Baumeisters were hit head-on. The driver of the little sports car and the Baumeisters were killed instantly. Investigating police confirmed the death of the crash victims, found out from the license plate of the wreck where the vehicle was registered, and sent the bodies of the couple to the morgue in Blauenwald for identification.

Viktor had no idea why Raphael knocked on his door early in the morning of April 27, a Sunday morning. Sleepily he inquired, "Yes, whatever it is, do you realize what time it is?" The clock next to him on his nightstand showed 5:00.

Raphael opened the door softly and said, "Sorry, Viktor, you must get up and go with me to the police station. I hate to tell you this, but your parents …," he stalled and Viktor became wide awake.

"What about my parents? Oh, my God, what happened?"

"They were traveling in Tuscany when their car …"

"Are they hurt?"

"I am so sorry to tell you …"

"How bad is it?"

"Viktor, brace yourself. They did not make it. Please get dressed and come with me. My car is in front of the gate."

After Viktor had collected himself, had put on some clothes, and followed Raphael to his car, he almost knew that the worst had happened. Silently they drove to the police station. The coroner was waiting for them and led them to the morgue where both bodies were lying stretched out beneath white sheets. Viktor was obliged to view both of them, and to verify that those mangled bodies were indeed of his parents. He hardly heard the consolatory words of the coroner. He was stunned and felt as if he were dreaming. They returned to the castle.

At the castle Raphael told Gerda the grim news and also went to the kitchen to inform *Frau* Grete. "Have a good drink sent up to Master Viktor's room—he needs it."

Soon everyone in the castle and at the village heard about the shocking news and a gloomy silence spread over Blauenwald. All *Frau* Grete could utter was, "So that's why those guys were so busy last night. I couldn't sleep a wink," referring, of course, to the *Spuk*.

Viktor, then thirty-three—still not finished with his education because he had interrupted his studies frequently to indulge his passions for travel, women, and wine—was the only heir; but he was neither willing nor capable of managing the estate at that time. He was now alone and had responsibilities to the staff in the castle and the villagers around Blauenwald. It hit him like a thunderbolt. For the first time in his life he could not just follow every one of his whims. In his despair he turned to his confessor, Raphael.

After his parents were laid to rest in the family vault, Viktor asked the priest for a consultation at the castle library. Here, surrounded by portraits of former castle owners, including his parents and grandparents, the two men had a serious conversation.

"Viktor, you asked me to talk with you. I know that you need to make decisions. How can I help?"

Viktor tried to hide his emotions but found it impossible to escape Raphael's stern, compassionate gaze. In a choked voice he replied, "I think you can help. I know that I have to change. I am now the owner of Blauenwald. The people here need to trust me. They don't have confidence in me now. I must turn my life around. Please, tell me what to do."

Raphael must have felt the great frustration of this man—so close to him in age—so recently bereft of both parents, all of a sudden facing great responsibilities, and finding himself at crossroads in his life. "The first thing I would advise you to do, Viktor, is to finalize your studies in Vienna and take over the management of the estate. You are lucky to have a capable manager now in Josef Wanz, but

I do not trust that man's intentions. He hardly ever attends church services and I find him evasive whenever I meet him. I believe that *Herr* Wanz had too much freedom when he was working for your parents. So I urge you to take over as master as soon as possible."

Viktor let this advice sink in. He thought for a long while. Raphael observed a gradual change in his friend's demeanor. Viktor's slouched posture straightened, his faltering hands quieted, and he looked at Raphael squarely. "You are right. I already had thought about going back to Vienna and completing my studies. I just needed to hear it from you. You did help me to make up my mind. Thank you, Raphael."

"One more thing," said Raphael. "I think you would gain much by approaching your parents' good friends, the Sattlers. Manfred is a very trustworthy person and his friendship would be a great asset for you. His son could be of help at the estate besides Sepp. And, oh, I want you to know that Adele and her son are doing well. She is grateful for your financial help."

Viktor nodded and got up. The two friends shook hands and parted.

* * *

A few weeks later Viktor returned to Vienna and resumed his studies. He finished his requirements for graduation. A year later he came back to Blauenwald to take over as owner of the estate. He found himself overwhelmed with the sudden changes that had happened to himself and his beloved home. He was utterly alone in the vast rooms and—being a gregarious, people-loving person—he soon realized that he needed company. He knew he had a drinking problem besides other deeply buried secrets. He also was aware of his dwindling funds. Instead of squandering money he had to learn to save.

He followed Raphael's advice and made friends with Manfred Sattler, proprietor of the large neighboring Weingut in Reichenfels that normally produced over 2000 gallons of Grün Veltliner (white wine) and about 500 gallons of Blauburger (red wine). Manfred had been the older Baumeisters' friend and confidant and after their deaths gladly extended this relationship to the son. He not only became Viktor's good friend, but also his advisor. His son, Paul, was younger than Viktor and had just finished studying viniculture in Graz. He had known Gerda from way back when both had gone to school together in Blauenwald, she several classes ahead of him. *He* fell deeply in love with Gerda, but *she* only had thoughts for her priest.

Since all the processing of the grapes raised at Blauenwald was done in Reichenfels, Viktor and Manfred had to meet frequently to do business. Manfred had lost his wife, Ursula, a few years before Viktor's parents died and he loved the company of the younger owner of Blauenwald Castle. His own sprawling house felt empty and not even his son could fill the void that Ursula had left. After the funeral of the Baumeisters he and Paul approached Viktor and invited him heartily to visit as often as he wished.

Not only did Viktor accept the fervent invitation to drop in at Reichenfels whenever he found the time, he also returned the hospitality and begged the Sattlers to consider Blauenwald estate their second home. Often Viktor and Manfred met at the *Buschenschank* (wine tavern) in the Blauenwald market place, and the village people observed the two wine growers engulfed in serious talk.

CHAPTER 3

Gerda

Still back in the early 1980s, like his parents, Viktor had trusted Sepp and Gerda Wanz to run the place. He, like Sepp Wanz, was a confirmed bachelor. However, unlike Sepp, Viktor had been enjoying his life and spending his parents' accumulated money. After his parents' sudden death and after Raphael had put a slight doubt about Sepp's motives into Viktor's mind, he knew that he had to take over the reins. He was not a child anymore. He was on the way to becoming a man with responsibilities.

Brother and sister Wanz reacted differently when the young master came back to Blauenwald Castle in 1981, settled in the rooms of his parents, and became the master of the castle. Almost overnight the former playboy changed into a man, cut back traveling, and seriously concentrated on managing the estate, now his. This did not sit well with Sepp Wanz, who had secretly hoped that Viktor would not be capable of taking care of the property. Instead of letting Sepp make major decisions, Viktor demanded that his manager had to report to him any changes he intended to implement. Sepp felt that his good times of free rein that he had enjoyed under Viktor's parents were over. He had liked the feeling of being in control and wished he were the owner of the estate. The premises were in optimal shape when the older Baumeisters died so suddenly. Sepp expected Viktor to let him continue managing the estate as if he were the owner, but was deeply disappointed when the heir apparent let him know that he intended to be the master by making several decisions that he, Sepp, found questionable. He found himself put back to his place as servant of the young "whippersnapper," as he considered the dawdling heir.

But Viktor was not the spoiled young man anymore that Sepp had wished him to be—the death of both parents had woken him up and he knew that his long extended childhood had ended abruptly. However, it was not easy for him to accept the fact that he was now the owner of the castle and had to act as model for the staff at the castle and the community of Blauenwald. He asked the parish priest, Raphael, to help him with the transition and to establish his authority. He still continued his drinking; though now he knew how to handle the consequences. He cut down his traveling and only visited California once in a while to stay with his relative, Erma Brenner, the first cousin of his mother, (Erma's and Susanne's fathers were brothers) and her family in Oakland, California. During those times Sepp had strict orders about how to run the estate in his absence. Also Manfred Sattler, now his friend and adviser, was authorized to visit Blauenwald and to report to Viktor about the state of affairs.

Sepp Wanz had his own agenda. Oblivious to the change in Viktor, now the owner of the estate, he would try to persuade his younger sister Gerda to woo Viktor. Why not—Gerda was past thirty and becoming an old maid. It was time to let go of that infatuation for the priest who, as he saw it, had no intention of ever looking at his sister in that way. Most people in Blauenwald agreed with Sepp that Gerda would make a good mistress of the castle.

Gerda, quite differently, welcomed the young heir to manage the estate and only hoped that he would find a wife soon so people might stop bothering her with the idea of marrying Viktor.

One rainy day after Viktor had taken over as master of Blauenwald and when nothing much could be done outside, Sepp invited Gerda to have a little *Jause* with him at his small house at the foot of "Castle Hill." Brother and sister were sitting at the kitchen table, a pitcher with lemon juice, two glasses, and a plate with sandwiches between them. Sepp filled their glasses and took a deep breath.

"Gerda, you are doing a good job as the housekeeper at the castle. I'd like you to become friendly with the new owner. Actually he is not so young anymore, being almost the same age as I. But he dallies away his life with travels and affairs and that has to stop. He also has a drinking problem. You would deal with all of that; I certainly think so. He is still inexperienced and not ready to take care of this estate. After more than ten years of work for young *Herr* Baumeister's parents I think that I know the ropes of running this place. We have to be very careful not to lose our good standing with Master Viktor. The estate is in good shape now and will stay that way if I can help it. I have to tell you this: I always dreamed of becoming the owner of a castle. Blauenwald is one of the most desirable estates in this area. The castle alone is worth a lot. Viktor ought to marry some day. There needs to be a mistress in the castle. If we play our cards right and you could convince Viktor to marry you, I'll be part of the family and might even buy him out some day. He is not used to staying around all year long and working hard from early morning till late evening as we do."

After this long harangue—he was not used to talking that much at one time—the squat little man took a long sip of fruit juice and stretched his limbs comfortably.

The young woman, wedged between her wishes to please her brother and to pursue her own dream of happiness, thought, *I see, that's why he asked me over*. She replied, "Ever since our parents died, you always wanted to run my life, Sepp. But I don't think I want to follow your advice this time. Master Viktor is a good man, but I don't love him. I like to work for him, but I could never marry him."

"I know that you have only eyes for that church man, Raphael. Gerda, I'm telling you, give up chasing after him. He is a devoted Catholic priest and he will never break his vows. He might like you, but he is dedicated to his church and will not give into your unhealthy cravings. You know I want the best for you. Give up that priest and try to make Viktor marry you. You two would make a good couple. Our future would be secure."

"I'm sorry, but my mind is made up," Gerda replied. "I don't care if I never marry. I know you want the best for me. Ever since our parents died and it's just you and I left, you have taken good care of me. But I am not a little girl anymore. And if I decide what to do with my life, that's my own affair. Please understand me, Brother."

She gave him a peck on the cheek, grabbed her jacket, and started to leave.

Sepp sighed. "If I can't talk sense into you, couldn't you at least look around at the young men in our village? I don't want you unhappy. You should be married and have a family before it's too late. By the way, you must know that young Paul Sattler from Reichenfels is sweet on you. Someday he'll inherit his father's estate. Raphael, even if he breaks his vows and marries you, has nothing. You would be as poor as a church mouse." He chuckled at his own pun.

Gerda was getting upset. "Please stop it, Sepp. I don't want to hear anymore of this." She put on her jacket, took her umbrella, opened the door, turned around once more and said, "You shouldn't talk. You aren't such a good example of being a family man. Why don't *you* get married? Now you'll have to excuse me. I have a million things to do. Thanks for the *Jause*."

With that she left, almost slamming the door behind her.

Sepp just shrugged his shoulders. *Women, who can figure them out?*

Sepp had a woman in his life, but she was just like a tool to him. Berta was a homely young female from Blauenwald Village. She did his housework and cooking and fulfilled his manly needs if summoned, nothing less, nothing more. She was doing it for the money. Her parents were divorced and she lived with her mother, a washer woman who worked for the castle. Not many feelings lost there.

Outside the rain was pelting.

After Gerda left, Sepp went back to his office to go over his correspondence. There were bills to pay, tools to order, and preparations for the grape harvest to take care of. The year had been good for all the crops and he had to hire help for the fall. He liked being busy. He also did some phone calls. He had some private business to attend to. But he couldn't help pondering. *Not much time to think about my foolish sister. She wants me to marry. Absurd! I'm better off by myself. Women only distract from work. I have enough trouble with Berta. But as long as I can avoid having to marry her, I'm okay. So far she knows that there is no such hope for that.*

Berta did not mind at all. Sepp was flattering himself thinking she might want to marry him. She came from a dysfunctional family and marriage was far from her mind, especially to a calculating man like Sepp. He paid her well and had always been good to her. That was enough for her. She was happy to have a good job.

It was still raining. Gerda walked up the linden alley leading to the castle gate, nodded a friendly greeting to Rupert, the gate-keeper, and slowly ascended the broad staircase to the upper floor. She agreed with her brother's wish to have Viktor married. Yes, the castle needed a mistress. *But—sorry, Brother, not me.* She knew that she could marry any young man in Blauenwald she wanted. She was a good-looking, well-poised woman, always dressed neatly, and of cheerful demeanor. Especially that Paul Sattler—he devoured her with his eyes whenever they met. But no one could take away her deep love for Raphael. And him she could not have. Would he ever change his mind? Was there a glimmer of hope? Her womanly intuition told her that her charms were not completely lost on him.

Resolutely she entered her room, put away her wet jacket and umbrella, donned her work apron and bandana, and resumed her duties.

Other people in Blauenwald had noticed that Paul had affections for the housekeeper at the castle. Whenever Gerda was shopping at the market and Paul happened to be around, he couldn't help staring at Gerda. She never did much more than return his friendly greet-ings. On Sunday mornings in church she listened transfixed to the sermons of the young priest and waited patiently in line to receive his warm handshake at the end of the service. It was obvious that Gerda did not love Paul and had only thoughts for Raphael.

Paul knew that Gerda did not love him, but he decided that, if he was ever going to be married, it had to be her. Patiently he waited for her and hoped that she would change her mind.

On a Sunday afternoon in Reichenfels, in the spacious kitchen of the manor house, Manfred and his son, Paul, made a little time for *Jause.* Paul was done with his studies now and looking for a job. Meanwhile he was helping his father and learning more about managing a *Weingut*.

"Anything planned for tonight, Paul?"

"No, I haven't made any plans. Maybe I'll just hit the sack and read a good book."

"Paul, I hate to see you fritter your life away. You should go out more often. Make dates with girls. Don't pine your youth away for Gerda. It's hopeless. At least that's what Viktor tells me. She loves that priest. Sepp also tells me that. He has dreams that Gerda would marry Viktor, but she is not interested. Neither is Viktor. Whenever he has a chance, he is off to America to be with his cousin Erma. Maybe he has a sweetheart over there? That castle needs a mistress. But so does our house."

Ever since Ursula Sattler had passed away, a few years before Alfred and Susanne had the fatal accident, Manfred had felt a big void in his home. Young Paul did not fill the place of his wife of fifty years. Manfred reconsidered his son's bachelor status when he looked at Paul's sad face.

He made one more pitch. "Paul, if you are so hung up on Gerda, you ought to go over to the castle and make a date with her. If you are persistent, maybe she'll give in. She is a nice enough young woman. And very industrious."

"Well, Father, you aren't telling me anything new. For me, Gerda is the only one. Some day Raphael will get his call to Rome and she'll notice me." Paul sighed, took his book, and disappeared to his room.

Wish something would happen there. Neither of them is getting any younger. Manfred took to mumbling to himself when he was alone. He was alone a lot. He brooded much. He looked at the situation at Blauenwald Castle the following way:

Manfred, after he became a widower, had been very close to Alfred and Susanne. The friendship started when Alfred's father, Rudolf, had come to Blauenwald in the early 1920s and had bought the castle, then for sale by its owner. Rudolf needed a secluded place in the country, where he could concentrate on his writing, rather than in Graz, the city where he had lived before, crowded in a small house with his family. Manfred knew about the scandal of Karl's birth and of Alfred's frustrated feelings when his mother was witnessing his father's unlawful affair with Maria, crying herself to sleep at night while those two were having a good time. Alfred was only eight years old when Karl was born in 1914 and Manfred was about Karl's age. When the old Baumeisters, Rudolf and Maria, had moved to Blauenwald as owners of the castle during the early 1920s, the two boys were eight years old and became good friends. They had met at school and liked each other.

Manfred remembered well when he had met Alfred Baumeister for the first time. It was at a Pathfinder event where the teenaged Alfred functioned as a leader of the two young boys. Sixteen-year-old Alfred, who spent his summers at Blauenwald, while going to boarding school for the rest of the year, first in Graz, later in Vienna, took Manfred and his brother Karl under his wing and the three of them became good friends. When World War II broke out in 1939, Karl, then twenty-five, joined the Army. The friendship of the two other boys deepened. Toward the end of the war both young men decided to get married: Manfred to Ursula who was an heiress of a *Weingut* in Reichenfels and Alfred to Susanne whom he had met on an excursion to Southern Germany. The weddings took place at the castle in Blauenwald. Karl's unfortunate death during the last year of the war cast a shadow over the lives of both couples.

After the weddings, the newlyweds stayed friends and saw each other often. It did not take long to get to each other's abodes on horseback or by carriage. Later there were cars to cover the two-kilometer distance. To both couples a son was born: Viktor at Blauenwald and several years later Paul at Reichenfels.

Still pondering the history of their friendship, Manfred thought that if Viktor would marry Gerda, as would have been an obvious solution to all problems—in this point agreeing with Sepp Wanz—Paul would get used to the idea that she was unavailable to him. And if Viktor did not marry Gerda and that priest would get a call to Rome and would leave Blauenwald, maybe she would come to her senses and marry Paul. Manfred liked her; she was a nice, capable young woman. She could make Paul happy. If only …!

Manfred sighed, put out his pipe, and went to bed also.

CHAPTER 4

Betty

Viktor was very secretive about his personal affairs. No one, not even Raphael, had an inkling of what was going on in faraway California, the main destination of Viktor's travels. His pretense was that he loved to visit with his dear relative Erma Brenner, a first cousin of his mother, Susanne. This close relationship had started in 1950 when he was just two years old and before Erma married Hans Brenner.

Erma was old enough to be his aunt, and this was what he called her, his "Aunt Erma." Erma and Susanne had been close and Susanne's son was very dear to her. The love was mutual and Viktor had often visited his "Aunt Erma," who lived in the small town of Bergen in southern Germany, which was not far from Blauenwald. Alfred and Susanne Baumeister had spent many happy weekends with Peter Fischer and his daughter Erma.

This close relationship lasted even when Erma met Hans Brenner during the war, married him, and immigrated to America in 1953. Viktor was only six when that happened. He wrote to his aunt as soon as he was taught to write, and Erma wrote back and sent pictures of her own children. During the late 1960s, as soon as Viktor was independent and able to travel, he started visiting the Brenners in California, got acquainted with the children, Heidi, eight years younger than he, Lotti, born in 1960, and Peter, a mere baby in 1967, and made it a habit to see his relatives at least once a year during the ski season. When Viktor suddenly became orphaned in 1980, his "Aunt Erma" and her family were a great consolation for him and helped him to cope with the tragedy.

Manfred was under the impression that the Brenners were the only attraction for Viktor in California. He had no idea that there was another person who aroused Viktor's interest. That person was Betty.

Viktor had met Betty, whose name was then Elisabeth Fromm Goldstein, first two years after his parents' demise at one of the Springlake storytelling meetings. The Springlake Storytellers' Circle had been kicked off by Fay Foster, the Brenners' neighbor at their mountain cabin in Springlake, a small community in the Sierra foothills. Hans and Erma Brenner had purchased their cabin in the late 1970s, and they had become friends with Bob and Fay. The Fosters were permanent residents at the lake, while the Brenners were weekenders. Hans worked as a mechanic at an auto shop, and Erma was a school teacher until their retirement during the mid '80s. They resided in Oakland, the heart of the Bay Area and only came up to the mountains on holidays and weekends. Other people lived around the lovely little lake that gave the community its name and formed a group called "The Lake Dwellers." Fay Foster and Erma Brenner had decided to ask several Lake Dwellers to start the tradition of storytelling. They were meeting at various Lake Dwellers' homes. At one of the first circle meetings the elderly Fromms, Mary and Luther, attended. They also brought their daughter Betty and her two sons, Nathan and Jacob. The Springlake Storyteller Circle had started in 1982 and was still going on while Viktor was pursuing his role as castle owner.

Viktor, who was visiting his relatives, and Betty, visiting her parents, attended those meetings. They couldn't help noticing each other. Listening to Viktor's story, Betty learned that Viktor owned a castle in Austria and that he was single. She was impressed. For the first time after the loss of her husband she became interested in a man again. She liked the handsome, muscular man in Austrian attire. Viktor listened to Betty's story and learned that she had been married to a Jewish man called David Goldstein who was killed in a car accident—similar to the way he had lost his parents—and that she had two young sons whom she was raising as a single parent. He admired her for that.

After a brief courtship they started thinking of marriage. Betty had told Viktor that she would consider becoming his wife if he not only would adopt her two boys, but also if she could keep her parents with her. She did not want to leave the two beloved people behind. Mary and Luther had wholeheartedly agreed to return to the old country with their daughter. Viktor was willing to do both and offered to let the elderly couple live with them at the castle. After all, there was plenty of room available. By the end of 1984 wedding plans had been made for June of the next year. The decision to leave her own country for good had not been easy for Betty. However, the advantage for her sons to have a father again and the obvious joy of her parents to return to Europe helped her to make up her mind.

Betty would make a definite change in Viktor's life. For the first time he was facing responsibility for more than himself. He now would have to care for a wife, two young boys, and two elderly parents-in-law. This added to the fact that he was now the owner and main decision-maker for a large estate, the representative person for the community, and the most important patron for the parish. Was he able to fulfill this image? He was not so sure.

All of this was on Viktor's mind when Manfred Sattler invited him for a little chat during the fall of 1984. It was a typical sunny and crisp Sunday afternoon in early November when the two friends were sitting together in Manfred's office in Reichenfels. Paul was working for his father at that time. Viktor was contemplating marriage plans but no one knew about this. After sharing each others' pleasure about the excellent harvest of this year's crops, their conversation switched to personal items.

"When are you going to California again, Viktor?" Manfred wanted to know.

"Most likely around Christmas and this time I'll stay away longer. I plan to be there until the end of June. In fact, Manfred, would you be so kind to look after the place once in a while and let me know how things are going? I know that the Wanzes will keep everything going smoothly, but I still would like you or Paul to come by occasionally."

Manfred was perturbed. He asked. "Are you still traveling around? I thought those days were gone. I know that you visit your cousin regularly, but for half a year?"

Viktor smiled mysteriously. He knew that he would persuade Betty to marry him since he had willingly agreed to her conditions. He looked forward to adopting the boys. The wedding, together with three other couples, all Lake Dwellers, had been set for June 15 in 1985 and he would surprise all of Blauenwald by coming home with a ready-made family. Not even Sepp and Gerda Wanz had an inkling yet. Not even Raphael. Nobody knew. He would inform Gerda just a week before bringing his new bride and her family with him, so the rooms at the castle would be ready for the guests.

"You'll see, Manfred. All will turn out for the best. Trust me." With that he got up, shook Manfred's hand, and left.

The friend went back to his paper work, wondering about what was going on in Viktor's life.

Betty officially accepted Viktor's marriage proposal on Christmas Eve in 1984. The two were sitting together in the cozy living room of the Fromm's cabin in the Sierra foothills. It was late in the evening. The Christmas tree was still lighted, outside snow was falling, and soft German music was playing on the radio. A few embers were still glowing in the fireplace. Mary and Luther had gone to bed.

"Would you like me to get another glass of eggnog?" Betty asked.

"Thanks, Betty, not right now. Right now I have more important things on my mind. First I want to give you a little present." He reached into his pocket and offered her a small box.

"Viktor, is this what I think it is?"

"Why don't you open it?"

Carefully she removed the festive wrapping, pried open the lid and saw it. Viktor watched her, smiling. Betty was delighted. She loved the ring. The weeks of indecision were over. She accepted Viktor's proposal and decided to take her new life in stride. The German ambience, the smell of the fresh-cut fir, the music from the European sender, and Viktor's love, so vividly expressed in his handsome face, convinced her—she was ready.

"Oh, Viktor, it's so beautiful. Yes, I will marry you. When will it be? Shall we wait for the others? Shall we all get married in June next year?" By "the others" Betty referred to three other couples to be married, all of them Lake Dwellers who had met during storytelling times.

"That would be great. It would give us enough time to get ready. I promise to never disappoint you." Viktor was very happy and meant what he said, at least at that moment.

The following six months went by fast and the big wedding took place as planned on June 15 in 1985. Shortly afterwards the newlyweds moved to Austria, together with the two young boys and the elderly parents.

* * *

Betty was not quite happy during her first year at Blauenwald. There were several reasons for this. She would never get over the loss of David. She felt like an outsider in Austria. The castle did not seem like home to her; it was too big, drafty, and cold in the winter and hot in the summer. The only consolation for her was that her boys and her parents were living with them also. She wanted to be a good wife to Viktor, but the people around her were so different. And Viktor was not at all like David. Also, she now was the mistress of a big estate. She had never been very fond of house or garden work, so David had hired help for that. Therefore she could concentrate on rearing her two sons and being a very good mother to them. She also could spend her free time working at the local library and reading. Her boys and her books were her whole world after the loss of her husband. She became a fulltime librarian with steady pay at the library where she was well-liked, so she was able to make an adequate living for her family.

At the castle she had to fill the role of mistress of a large household.

Viktor knew from the beginning that Betty was a very serious person. She did not seem to have any vices. Somehow he knew that he needed someone like her. He was tired of purposeless traveling. She would be a steadfast, reliable force in his life. When he met Betty in 1982, he realized that she was still mourning the loss of her husband. She was not ready then to pay attention to his advances. It would take time. Only a few months later—after she had heard that he, Viktor, had lost both his parents, and also in a senseless automobile accident like the one that killed David—was he able to get closer to her and to convince her that she would have a good future with him in Austria.

During the first month of her stay in Austria, Viktor took Betty to the *Buschenschank* in the market place in Blauenwald. That beer tavern was the most popular meeting place in the village and Betty observed how crowded and noisy the rustic public house was. Viktor had led her to a quieter corner, but soon the two were surrounded by loud-voiced countrymen, all curious about the new mistress at the castle. When the banker, manager of the *Österreichische Bank,* Hermann Reich, and the mayor of Blauenwald, Gottlieb Hausmann, both accompanied by their chatty wives, entered and headed directly to the corner where Viktor and Betty were sitting, the crowd parted respectfully. The two men asked politely if they might join the Baumeisters. They sat down and ordered a round of beer for everyone. The mayor said in his booming voice, "Well, Viktor, look at you. A married man now. Congratulation! How do you like it here in our Austria, *Frau* Baumeister?" He lifted his giant *Bierstein* toward the couple and Viktor heartily clicked his tumbler with the banker's. The two wives looked at Betty curiously and seemed to enjoy their beer. They whispered to each other. Betty cringed. She could hardly understand what the mayor said over the noise around them. She turned to Viktor for help. Viktor felt sorry for her.

"Thanks, Gottlieb. Betty is still learning to speak German. So far she likes it fine in our country." He emptied his mug and winked to the waiter to bring another round. He started to get red in his face and his voice became louder. Betty didn't touch her beverage and felt very frustrated. She did not like beer and felt out of place among all the noise. Viktor was a little disappointed, but hoped that in time Betty would learn to appreciate Austrian fellowship.

Now it was Hermann Reich's turn to toast the newlyweds. But Betty had enough. She motioned to Viktor that she was ready to leave. Reluctantly he excused himself and Betty and took her home. "Sorry it was so noisy. That's our Austrians for you; they love crowds." Betty remained quiet.

She was aware of Viktor's drinking problem. He also loved his tobacco. There was hardly anything she could do about that. Everyone around them smoked, especially the men. This was Europe. But she did not know that Viktor had a deep-rooted secret, something he never talked about. Though she sensed that there was something he had not told her, she never pried. She wanted to love him. But she could not help comparing him to her former husband. How different was he from David! David and she had talked about everything. There were no secrets. They had lived in nearly total harmony. They were similar in their habits, liked to read, and seldom went outside. Viktor, on the other hand, loved the outdoors and physical work. He was unhappy about the fact that Betty was not enjoying her status as mistress of the castle. He wanted her to be loved by everybody in the castle and the village. Instead, during the first year of their marriage Betty was not very popular with the people in Blauenwald. They could not understand her, though she tried hard to master the Austrian dialect, so different from the classical German that she had learned in high school back in her native town in California. The Austrian country people mistook Betty's shyness for haughtiness and even laughed behind her back.

They, like Josef Wanz, and even Manfred Sattler, who knew that his son pined in vain for the young woman, would have liked it better if Viktor had married Gerda who got along splendidly with the town folks and always had a friendly word for the simple people. While Gerda was one of them, Betty was a stranger.

Also the way Betty dressed did not make her very popular. She preferred drab colors: browns, grays, dark blues, and blacks—even in summer. Viktor had tried to interest her in wearing *dirndl* dresses, those colorful outfits featuring gaily printed skirts, white blouses, tight-fitting vests, and an apron. But she hesitated. Maybe some day?

Gerda, on the other hand, practically lived in *dirndl* dresses and owned a whole assortment of these rustic garments. When she strutted through the village, brimming with youthful energy, greeting people left and right, shaking their hands warmly, and looking deep into their eyes, always having something nice to say, they felt uplifted. Young village males tried to approach her. Paul Sattler from Reichenfels was seriously in love with her, but was rebuffed like all the others.

She, Gerda, had feelings only for the village priest.

While Sepp was deeply disappointed about Viktor's choice of a bride, Gerda welcomed Betty warmly. She had loved and respected the former castle owners and brought the same unwavering loyalty to the young master. This loyalty was transferred to the new mistress of the castle. Gerda was getting on in age and her brother had wanted to see her married, preferably to Viktor, which would have brought him one step closer to his dream of owning the castle one day. He knew about her infatuation with Raphael. He did not take this too seriously. In his point of view nothing could go wrong with making his foolish sister see the futility of her expectations. But he did not count on Gerda's steadfastness or "stubbornness," as he saw it. What he did not realize was that he was just as stubborn in pursuing his wish to become castle owner some day.

Gerda did not fall in love with Viktor and never would. Her heart was occupied and for the time being no one could take Raphael Garibaldi's place in this seat of affections. She had met him first in the early 1970s, when he was elected by the congregation of Blauenwald to serve as their priest. The old priest—who had lived in the east wing of the castle—was ready to retire and the parish needed a successor. She was barely twenty then. Deeply religious, at first she kept her feelings for her priest to herself and only confessed a while later when she was employed as housekeeper at the castle and had to endure the closeness of his living quarters—right next to her room, separated from him by just a thin wall.

Unlike some of the other people of Blauenwald, Gerda liked Betty from the beginning. One morning, still in 1985—a few months after the young Baumeisters' arrival—Gerda was checking the work of her two assistants, Hanni and Erika. She walked through the rooms, dust cloth in hand, to see that all the furniture had been properly cleaned. When she entered the library, she encountered Betty, seated comfortably in one of the velvet covered armchairs and engulfed in a book. Gerda had admired her new mistress from the minute she laid eyes on her. She, as most others in Blauenwald who had heard that Viktor had married an American, had expected someone resembling an image of a stereotype, gleaned from watching television and American movies: flashy, spoiled, loud-mouthed, dressed in the newest fashion, and loaded with expensive jewelry. How little did Betty fit this expectation! She was plain, somberly attired, wore no make-up, spoke little and when she did, with an exact pronunciation. A little accent, of course. Her knowledge and love of books, English as well as German, amazed Gerda who only had had elementary schooling. And German was not even Betty's native language!

She apologized for not having knocked before entering, but Betty invited her in with a friendly smile. "Come in, *Fräulein* Wanz."

Gerda, knowing well the difference in status between her and the new mistress, would have liked some friendly conversation. But she was not quite ready for the intimate chat that Betty was offering. Reluctantly, she started cleaning one of the already dusted shelves. She was surprised when Betty closed her book and addressed her.

"Good morning, Gerda, I see that you are already working hard this early. Are those shelves really so dirty that they need cleaning?"

Gerda turned around and smiled. "Not really, *Gnädige Frau*," she said haltingly.

Betty returned the smile. "I thought so. Why don't you drop the charade? Let's have a nice talk. I have the feeling both of us are lonesome and need to chat a little."

"Oh no, Gnä' … *Frau* Baumeister. What would people say, if they knew?"

"My husband and your brother are working outside, so what 'people' are you talking about?"

Gerda put her cloth carefully onto a little table and stepped over to Betty's chair. She sat down on the little footstool and looked up to Betty's face. "Your husband wouldn't mind so much, but my brother; he'd kill me," she whispered, looking around as if she was afraid that Sepp would enter the library any minute.

"Oh no, Gerda." Betty said boldly, although she knew that she was stepping over a line, created by the men running the affairs of the castle. "Your brother wants the best for you. What could he possibly have against us two talking together?"

"Well, for one thing, you are the mistress of the castle and I am only the housekeeper. But then, you don't know much about what's going on here, do you?"

"I guess I don't. Could you please tell me, Gerda? And please, call me Betty, I would love that."

Gerda looked horrified. "Oh no, Gnä … *Frau* …." She swept her eyes around the room again, but presently straightened up, smiled at her mistress, and said frankly, "Why not? I'd love to call you Betty. But …," and she let her shoulders fall again, "in America this would probably be okay, but here in Austria—things are different. Housekeepers just don't talk to their bosses like they are family. It's just not done and even your husband wouldn't like it. And, maybe—" she looked up to Betty shyly, "maybe that's why the people in the castle and the village don't like you so well. You're so different— Betty," she said, feeling bolder. "I could teach you some things that would help you get more friends around here. You are such a great person, so educated, so…," she put her face into her hands and almost started crying. "So much better than all of us here. I just can't explain, but I don't want you to get hurt."

"Why would anyone want to hurt me, Gerda?" Betty laid her hand on Gerda's shoulder. "Come on, look at me. I am so glad that you told me you like me. That's enough for me. I guess it would be better not to aggravate the other people. After all, I *am* intruding here and should not try to change your customs. But whenever you and I are alone like right now, let's be friends. On the outside, we still are mistress and housekeeper, I understand that now."

Gerda nodded and stood up, picked up the dust cloth, and resumed her work. After a while she looked back and observed that Betty was absorbed in her book again. She smiled happily and quietly left the room, shutting the door noiselessly.

In the hall she met Hanni, one of her staff.

"*Fräulein* Wanz, please, where is the *Gnädige Frau*? *Frau* Schwarz needs to know what kind of meat she wants for dinner."

"That's fine, Hanni, I'll go down to the kitchen. *Frau* Baumeister is working in the library and doesn't want to be disturbed." She handed the dust cloth to the girl and told her, "You could go to the Rittersaal and dust everything there. It hasn't been done for ages. Be sure not to forget anything. I'm going to check."

"Okay," Hanni replied and thought to herself, *What kind of work would that be, early in the day in the library? If our Gnädige Frau would only take this cloth and do a little work around here.*

She shrugged her shoulders and went to the *Rittersaal*.

Gerda walked down the back stairs to the roomy kitchen.

This was *Frau* Grete's territory. *Frau* Margarete Schwarz, Grete for short, hired by Maria Baumeister as housekeeper right after they took over the castle in the early 1920s, was now, after Gerda Wanz took over as housekeeper, the cook and the authority of the large castle kitchen. Both *Frau* Grete and *Fräulein* Gerda were living on the second floor in the east wing of the castle. *Frau* Schwarz's husband, Fritz, sick now and confined to a wheelchair, had been the factotum, fixing whatever was broken on the premises. He stayed most of the time in the Schwarzes' apartment watching television or gazing out the window. The view from the east wing windows was directed toward the Hungarian plains. Not at all like the Alpine vista toward the west or the view of lovely hills southward. The older Baumeisters had built a ramp for his wheelchair, leading from the second floor to the ground, on the outside of the east wing. Now Luther Fromm took over being the "factotum." Later, when crippled by arthritis, he would also take over using the wheelchair ramp after Fritz Schwarz's death.

Frau Grete Schwarz was a psychic. She heard noises that others didn't hear and she liked to convince others that there was a *Spuk* haunting the castle. The year before Viktor's parents were killed, she had reported to her faithful listeners—mostly the young helpers in the kitchen and house—that the noises in the attic, like shuffling feet and low moans, were louder than usual. Her audience became scared. After the sudden, unexpected death of Alfred and Susanne the noises calmed down again and *Frau* Grete did not predict anymore calamities. However, in 1984, when the young master left for California, she reported to her willing audience that the *Spuk* had stepped up again. "This time there are even bumps like somebody was dancing. Even squeaky sounds like a baby crying! Something's going to happen soon."

She proved to be right. Something did happen.

What happened was Viktor's return to Blauenwald with an entire family in tow, and then a brand-new baby was expected to be born in May of 1986. Soon everyone was so busy with these new events that there was no time for gloomy thoughts, and even *Frau* Grete had no time to listen to the activities of the mysterious *Spuk*.

When Gerda entered the kitchen, a flurry of activities went on. It was close to *Mittagessen,* the main meal of the day around noon, and *Frau* Grete's two helpers from the village and Gerda's assistant, Erika, were busy preparing the meal. At the stroke of twelve o'clock one of the workers was banging on the large gong by the door with a wooden mallet and the first hungry workers started mulling into the staff dining room through the door toward the inside court yard. They had been raking and weeding the ground under the huge linden tree and they appreciated the appetizing smell wafting through the entire first floor.

Frau Grete ruled here. The kitchen was huge. A giant coal-burning stove, shelves loaded with crockery, utensils hanging on the walls, a massive wooden work table surrounded by wooden stools standing in the middle. Long years of cooking had blackened the walls and ceiling, and even repeated whitewashing did not cover the smoky tinge. In the morning the kitchen helpers were sitting around the large oaken work table, scrubbing, peeling, and dicing vegetables for *Mittagessen*. A big pot with soup was steaming on the stove and several loaves of freshly baked bread were ready to be sliced on the marble cutting table. *Frau* Schwarz always sent the menu to Gerda who in turn presented it to Betty, who usually nodded absentmindedly when she looked it over. Most of the time Betty did not care about the food—so new and strange to her. But she had learned to like the many varieties of *Knödels* (dumplings) of different ingredients. She also liked the various casseroles and main entrees. She changed the menu seldom. Only when certain soups, like anything made from raw blood, were on the menu, did she shake her head. It was the blood that was revolting to her. Soon *Frau* Schwarz found out that Betty preferred raw vegetables and salads. Spinach, for instance—when overcooked and almost atomized by a grinder—she found impossible to accept.

A typical conversation between Betty and *Frau* Grete during the first months after the young mistress had arrived would go like this:

"Please, *Frau* Schwarz, just cut the fresh spinach into small pieces, don't grind it, and only cook it only for a few minutes. Please don't add any water; this fresh vegetable from the garden is almost good enough to be eaten raw." And *Frau* Grete would shake her head and resign.

"If you say so, Gnädige *Frau*."

When Gerda entered the kitchen, *Frau* Grete greeted her and invited her to sit down. Gerda looked at the menu. "Steamed spinach?" she asked.

Frau Schwarz shrugged her shoulders. "The new mistress just wants everything not fit for humans to eat," she complained to Gerda who tried to sooth her.

"Relax, Grete, I like the way she wants you to cook. The vegetables lose their taste if cooked too long. It's much healthier if they are still crisp. Just bear with her. She is really a nice person."

"If you say so, Gerda." *Frau* Grete mumbled to herself. She took a small pottery casserole dish, put in the heap of spinach that had just been washed, dried and cut by one of the kitchen helpers, and deposited it onto the side of the stove. In a few minutes the large pile of greens had condensed into a small mound of leaves, looking appetizing and smelling delicious. *Frau* Grete was still skeptical. "Food fit for rabbits," she growled.

But she was pleased when Betty came into the kitchen after the meal, thanking her. "I am so grateful to you, *Frau* Schwarz, for your efforts. I loved the way you prepared the spinach today." So Gerda served as a liaison between the two worlds in the castle, the upstairs and the downstairs. She managed to get along well with both.

During the first year at Blauenwald, Betty was still shy around the staff members. One criticizing look from *Frau* Grete, even from the helpers, made her uneasy. Those accomplished people, who had been doing their work for many years—before Betty became their mistress—did not take easily to changing their habits. It took flexibility on both sides to get along.

"Glad you liked it, hope your husband did too." *Frau* Schwarz was not so sure that he did. He was used to *her* cooking; and so was everybody else in the castle. *Frau* Baumeister's parents, of course, were also Americans and liked their food half cooked, but they were so sweet and compatible and got along with all the people at the castle. Even the villagers liked them better than the young mistress.

Next to the kitchen, which sprawled underneath the entire upper west wing, was the dining room for the staff. During the mid 1980s the staff consisted of around fifteen workers. Half of them were working outside, in the vineyards, the gardens, and the forest. The other half worked in the castle—kitchen staff supervised by *Frau* Schwarz and housemaids under the authority of Gerda Wanz, Rupert, the night watch, and also the washerwoman and her daughter Berta, who came up from the village once a week for washing and another day for ironing. All these helpers ate in the large dining room, sitting on long benches before long tables. At noon the huge gong in front of the kitchen sounded twelve times and hungry workers came from all the parts of the estate. Usually someone from the kitchen staff operated that gong.

Fräulein Wanz and *Frau* Schwarz were invited to eat upstairs with the castle owners and the village priest. This was not the usual etiquette in Austrian castles, and both, Gerda and Grete, did not take advantage of it often. But Viktor felt that the era of his parents was over and that it was time for new rules. Betty agreed in this matter wholeheartedly.

Though also invited to eat with the owners, Sepp Wanz preferred eating by himself in his little house. His girlfriend Berta prepared his meals.

The parents Fromm blended in perfectly and the boys had each other during the long meals. *Frau* Schwarz had trained her staff well and the food always came up to the upstairs' dining room through the dumbwaiter, piping hot. Two of the kitchen staff took care of delivering the food while the third one served the meal at the table. The upper dining room was next to the verandah, outfitted with nice *Meissen* china in handcrafted cabinets, sturdy trays, arrays of crystal, and a large oval mahogany table with matching chairs, upholstered with silky material. The large picture window looked out toward the west. In the distance the white capped Alps made a picturesque view.

Next to the dining room was the library, still dating from the times of Viktor's grandfather, the writer. He had also been a collector of books. Valuable first editions of classics filled one shelf; many more shelves were stocked with reading material of various genre. This was Betty's favorite room—she could spend hours here, reading to her heart's content. Adjacent was the sitting room, outfitted with old-fashioned armchairs and a large sofa facing the fireplace. On one of the inner walls stood an old spinet piano, which the older Goldstein boy, Nathan, loved to play. The same lovely view of the mountains through large windows enhanced these two rooms.

Viktor had chosen the room adjacent to the sitting room to be his study. It used to be just a spare room. Above his desk of solid German oak hung the picture of his grandfather Rudolf in his younger years, with a small goatee, well groomed, and a happy countenance.

On the corner of the west and north wings was the tea room, a charming place with windows on the two outer walls. Only very distinguished guests were invited into this little gem to enjoy the special fineries from *Frau* Grete's kitchen, delicately flavored teas, special coffees, and home baked goods. *Frau* Schwarz had been trained at the famous Sacher café in Vienna and her creations were always delicious. One of her cookbooks on the shelf above her desk in the kitchen was Katharina Prato's *Der Große Prato*, a thick volume featuring all of the recipes that the famous *Kochbuchautorin* (author of cookbooks) had collected during her long life. No wonder her husband, Eduard Pratobevera, died of stomach ailments.

Betty could never adjust her simple eating habits to the richness of Austrian cooking. In her home country she was used to shopping sparingly, using very little meat, being careful with starches, and preferring steamed vegetables. For Austrians this was a diet fit for rabbits. Fresh salads, something Betty loved with every meal, were heavily laced with *Kernöl*, bacon bits, and pure cream. Viktor loved the calorie-rich meals and became concerned that Betty was starving herself.

The elderly parents of Betty occupied a comfortable apartment on the southeast corner on the upper floor of the castle. It consisted of a living room, kitchen, bedroom, and bath and both Betty and Viktor had done everything possible to make Mary and Luther Fromm feel at home.

They had been raised in the Lutheran faith, had tolerated the fact that Betty's first husband had been Jewish, and now had become diligent Catholics. This was truly demonstrating the flexibility and tolerance of these two octogenarians.

Their two rooms had a fireplace, which was necessary during the harsh winters. The living/dining room was on the corner, with large picture windows toward east and south. A small kitchen had been installed next to the dining area and Mary could prepare *Frühstück* and a light *Abendbrot* in her own home. The entire apartment was sunny and friendly. This establishment was next to the bell tower of the little church and every workday morning at six o'clock the bells tolled beautiful tunes. Fortunately the Fromms were used to getting up early and they loved this melodic wake-up call. On Sundays the bells started an hour later and presented a wonderful concert.

Mary and Luther had adjusted well to their new home.

They were invited to share *Mittagessen* with the rest of the family in the comfortable dining room next to the verandah in the west wing.

Sometimes Mary felt like doing some work around the house and had asked *Frau* Schwarz and Gerda if she could help them. This offer was gladly accepted and often Betty would meet her mother in the hallway, dressed in housedress and bandana, on her way to the kitchen, or doing some dusting in the staterooms. Mary's own apartment was quickly taken care of in the morning, since both Luther and she were early risers and were used to having their living quarters in order before most member of the household were stirring. Luther liked to read his paper—delivered every morning by the mailman—to smoke his pipe, and to take a little walk in the garden and to the vineyard. Whenever he detected something that needed fixing, he tried to help. At home he used to putter at his workbench and he liked to do the same here. Viktor and Sepp appreciated this willingness of the elderly couple to do their share of work and so did the other workers. Everyone liked them. While Fritz Schwarz, *Frau* Grete's husband, was still alive, Luther and he visited each other frequently and had good talks.

Mary was a real confidant for many of the castle people. The fact that she was raised in Germany and spoke their language fluently played an important role. Betty had learned the language in school and had difficulties expressing herself. Her German was a little bookish. People didn't understand her very well.

Next to the Fromms' apartment in the south wing was the master bedroom and next to that were two small guestrooms. A windowless storage room was behind the bell tower of the church. The east wing was occupied by the boys' room, several more guestrooms, the Schwarz's apartment, Gerda's, and the priest's rooms. All those faced the morning sun. All the rooms had running water; a luxury that had been installed in the 1970s after the economy had been recovered from the perils of the war.

Situated on the southwest corner of the upper floor was the spacious verandah, the gathering place for the castle owners, their relatives, and occasional friends. A tall spruce tree with spreading branches provided necessary shade during the sweltering afternoon hours in summer. In the evening a gentle breeze felt refreshing. Here the family met—weather permitting—relaxed, and had small meals.

(The large meal at noon was always served at the dining room.) The verandah was furnished with a sturdy round table surrounded by weather proofed chairs. Comfortable wooden swing-sofas placed around the low verandah walls allowed a good-sized group to gather here. *Frau* Grete took care of providing the assembled people with nourishment and drinks.

Sepp and Gerda usually did not join the family gatherings on the verandah. Both were occupied with their managing chores, Sepp outside, Gerda inside. Raphael, on the other hand, had more leisure time to join the family. They all enjoyed the company of the learned man.

The priest didn't know about Gerda's affection for him until she told him during confession time in 1975. It was troublesome for the young man who had committed himself to celibacy. Gerda was a healthy, beautiful young woman and only separated from him by a fairly thin wall. He needed all his strength and determination not to break his vows and quench all budding feelings of attraction. However, he felt that the closeness of their living quarters was a temptation sent from God to strengthen his faith. He avoided meeting with Gerda as much as possible. Until 1975 he had been oblivious to the charms of all young women at the castle and the village, which must have broken more than one heart in the community since he was a well-built, slender and handsome man, a powerful preacher, and he radiated love to everyone. He only began noticing Gerda after she had confessed her love to him. From now on Raphael concentrated on staying in good repute with his archbishop in Rome. The sooner he would be called to serve in Rome to further his career within the church, the better. It would take several years until the desired call from Rome might be coming, enabling Raphael to leave Blauenwald and to advance his career. Therefore Manfred and Paul Sattler were not the only ones who prayed for Raphael's call to Rome.

CHAPTER 5

Sepp

Josef Wanz felt thwarted when Viktor came home married and he had to bury his plans to become Viktor's brother-in-law. But he still did not give up his dream to become the owner of Blauenwald Castle some day. He had to find another way. It became important to him to make enough money in order to buy the estate some day. Sepp resented more and more that he was put in his place as manager and servant of the castle owner. He did not like the new mistress. All the control over his management did not sit well with him and he developed a deep-seated hatred toward Viktor. His burning desire to own Blauenwald Castle one day grew stronger. But he was able to disguise these feelings so that nobody became suspicious except his sister. However, Gerda had her own problems. Viktor seemingly trusted him. Betty, in her friendly way, welcomed him at the castle, but felt some animosity.

Nobody was prepared for the breaking news about the scandal Sepp was entangled in when the ugly news broke.

Grazer Nachrichten, 13ten Oktober, 1985
Austrian Wines Pulled off Shelves

The trial of five Austrians, Richard and Jeramia Westheimer, Otto Kreiser, Franz Aschenbach, and Josef Wanz will take place on January 15, 1986, at the Royal Court House in Vienna. In 1980 this group of perpetrators had conspired to concoct the producing of artificial wines that almost brought the lucrative Austrian wine business to a standstill. Bottles of Austrian wines had to be pulled off shelves all over the world. After discovery of the crime, all participants in the scandal pled guilty to diluting 1.5 million gallons of wine with an antifreeze ingredient, diethylene glycol, for sweetening. They sold the tainted wines for high prices all over the world. They also manufactured artificial wines, which proved poisonous. While the doctored wines only caused illness, the artificial wines were confirmed to be deadly.

This newspaper article on the front page of the *Grazer Nachrichten* was lying on the round table on the verandah. On a pleasant Sunday afternoon during fall in 1985 the family was enjoying the cool breeze on the verandah. It was about four months after Viktor had brought his wife and her family home to his castle. Viktor had come in from the vineyard for a *Jause*, because he was hungry from physical work and needed some little in-between meal. Manfred Sattler had just joined the group and Mary and Luther were ensconced on one of the comfortable swing-sofas. Betty had her sewing basket beside her and was working on some clothes for the baby, expected in spring of 1986. The boys, ten-year-old Nathan and seven-year-old Jacob, were sprawling on the floor, engrossed in a game of *Schwarzer Peter*, similar to the American "Old Maid." They had just come from the village school and needed a rest. The men, Viktor, Manfred, and Luther, were talking about the sad tidings concerning Sepp Wanz.

"What's the news about Sepp, Viktor? Heard anything about the trial?" Manfred asked. He had come over on his horse for a short visit between working hours. He saw the newspaper lying on the table and studied the headlines.

"Not too much, Manfred. The hearing is set at the middle of January next year. Meanwhile your son is taking good care of the grounds. That young man sure has learned a lot working for you and he's using his lessons from the academy very well. Unless there is a serious drought coming this fall, our vines will produce a bumper crop."

"Tell me about *Herrn* Wanz's dilemma. I only heard rumors. What was really going on? I always thought that he was such an excellent manager," Luther joined the conversation.

Just when Viktor was ready to start this controversial topic, Raphael entered the verandah and was heartily invited to join the group.

"I just heard Luther mentioning Sepp's name. I too would like to hear more about why your manager is involved in a criminal investigation. Or is this a sensitive issue?"

"Yes and no, Raphael and Luther." Viktor stuffed his pipe and started to inhale deeply. Betty looked at him sadly. She did not like his smoking and drinking, but was still learning to tolerate both. She was clever enough to know that it is not easy to change a person's habits.

Viktor started explaining what was happening to his manager.

"You might have heard about the wine-scandal going on during the beginning 1980s. Manfred, I know you were very concerned when many Austrian winemakers, in fact wine merchants from all over the world, had to pull their bottles from the shelves because of a scandalous conspiracy. In case you haven't read the article here," he pointed to the newspaper on the table, "a group of Austrian winemakers had gotten together and had conspired a massive wine-tainting operation to make profits. The bottled concoctions were sold all over the world. Well, after some of the people who drank the stuff got ill and one even died, those scoundrels were found out and investigated. Those four wine tainters were almost household names at that time. Recently one of them leaked Sepp's name. He had been a silent partner before the news broke.

"So, Sepp wanted to make some money on the side. We had no idea about this, just learned about it when they took him to jail on Monday morning. This is very disappointing and it's why I had asked Paul to take over here at Blauenwald. The trial will start in a few months, on January 15 of next year. Meanwhile they'll keep all those suspects, including Sepp, in the country jail. If pronounced guilty, they will face prison sentences. If Sepp can defend his actions, and I'll see to it that he has a good lawyer, he'll be back. But I do not trust him with the entire estate anymore. He'll have Paul to work by his side."

Viktor looked at Manfred and his friend nodded his head.

"Who would have thought of that? Our dependable Sepp!" Then, turning to Betty, he asked, "Does Gerda know?"

Gerda and Sepp didn't see each other very often. Both were fully occupied and Sepp did not take his meals at the castle.

"I don't think so, didn't you tell her?" she asked Viktor.

"I did not, and neither did anyone else, unless someone from the outside told her." Viktor replied.

Manfred looked gravely at the men and said, "Most likely Paul told her. He is rather close to her and he, without doubt, knows why Viktor asked him to substitute for Sepp for the time being."

Viktor agreed. "It's possible, Manfred."

At this point *Frau* Grete entered with a large tray laden with a good *Jause*. There were tempting foods on that tray, *Semmeln* with butter and jam, delicious sugar cookies, and even pieces of *Sacher Torte*, coffee, tea, and a carafe of *Heuriger* wine. Betty frowned slightly. She did not approve of all that in-between food only two hours after a substantial meal of *Knödels* and *Sauerbraten*. Also drinking wine and beer in the middle of the day worried her. She herself did not drink at all. She had to think of the little newcomer in her womb. David and she had never taken any alcohol.

Viktor was slightly disappointed at his wife's rather Spartan habits. He thought that she might change. But maybe she was right. It would be better if he stayed away from alcohol. However, this was Austria, and Austrian vintners ought to be allowed to enjoy their own products. Betty was too strict! *But she is such a good person,* he kept telling himself.

Lovingly he looked at his wife, busily preparing for their baby. In her somber clothes—she still preferred wearing browns, blacks, and grays, her hair put up in a simple bun, and not wearing any make-up—she surely did not look Austrian yet. She had not changed since he fell in love with her almost three years ago. She looked so different from Gerda and *Frau* Grete in their colorful *dirndl* outfits. Maybe Gerda should go shopping with her for a new wardrobe? *How well do I really know my Betty?* he asked himself.

After *Frau* Grete had served the men with her tempting dishes and drinks, she left the verandah silently and returned to do her chores. She smiled to herself. While the men needed an in-between-meal though they had a nourishing *Mittagessen* just a few hours ago, the women were hardly ever hungry in the afternoon. They had silently shaken their heads when Grete motioned with her hands, if they wanted to be served with a little *Jause* also. Both, *Frau* Marie (the name she always wanted to be addressed by) and *Frau* Betty, certainly could afford to put some meat on their bones. How could they resist her culinary delicacies? And wasn't eating the most important thing in life? It surely was for her! *Frau* Schwarz's stately figure—pressed into a colorful *dirndl* hardly obscuring her over-flowing corpulence—was a sure indication that she took several *Jauses* a day.

The sun was almost down now and dusk would be setting in shortly. Manfred and Raphael thanked Viktor for the *Jause* and left. Viktor also got up, kissed Betty briefly on the cheek, and went to his office next to the library in the west wing. He sat down at his desk and pondered about the events that had taken place before.

He remembered how grateful he was to have Sepp Wanz taking care of Blauenwald Castle and lands after his parents' death. He knew then that, in order to become a good master, he had to change. He also had to know more about the people working for Blauenwald Castle. And then he had to take Sepp a peg down from the pedestal he had stood upon before. He would never forget the day when he became suspicious about Sepp's motives to work for him.

In the beginning of 1981 a serious conversation between both of them had taken place in this very room; with his grandfather Rudolf looking jauntily down at them from the portrait hanging above the big oak desk. The manager had already been involved in the wine-tainting scheme, but no one knew about it then.

"Sepp, can you continue working for me, I mean now that I am the owner of the castle estate?" Viktor had asked, almost begging the squat, robust little man, so sure of himself, so different from him, Viktor, and so competent.

"What are you saying, Viktor?" Sepp was only one year older than Viktor, but it seemed that he, Sepp, had far more years behind him. "Of course I'm staying. Your father would have never allowed me to let you down. Of course, there will be more work now around here. Work that your father did behind the scenes and that you don't know much about. I would like to ask you if you will let me take over the handling of the financial affairs, so you don't have to bother about anything and can continue your life as you like it. There is only one thing I'll ask from you."

"And what is that, Sepp?" Viktor felt somewhat belittled by the demanding voice. His instinct told him to be aware of being handled as an incompetent youngster.

"You will give me full power of attorney so I can make my own decisions."

Viktor perked up. This was a dangerous moment. He knew that he still needed Sepp, but Sepp wanted to take over the reins. He thought for a long while, during which time his manager sat squarely and quietly and shifted his cap from one hand to the other. Finally Viktor spoke up,

"*Herr* Wanz," he said sternly, making Sepp look up slightly ruffled, "I will not do such thing. I shall finish my studies in Vienna and after my graduation I will start taking over the management of *my* estate. *I* will be able to follow in my father's footsteps." And he added, "With your help."

He remembered well the rush of adrenalin in his veins. It was a wonderful feeling. Sepp got up, put on his cap and left without saying another word. Viktor had turned over a new leaf and it was clear that Sepp could not do a thing about it. However, from then on the friendly relationship between the two men had suffered a crack. Viktor, though honoring Sepp's expertise, had begun to doubt his loyalty.

Now, almost five years later, Viktor was fully convinced that he had reacted correctly then, in 1981. Betty told him that same evening of October 13, 1985, when the newspaper article had come out, that Dr. Amato had warned her about Sepp during one of his visits at the castle. She had asked him how he knew about these rumors, since she felt that all of this seeming scandal sounded like so much gossip.

"I hear things," the doctor had answered ominously.

Betty decided to share this bit of news with her husband.

Viktor had followed through with his decision to change his ways. Within a year he graduated from the academy and took over the management of the estate. All of Blauenwald Village was interested in the events at the castle. Though Viktor's reputation had been and still was tarnished by rumors about his excessive lifestyle and that there might be an illegitimate child somewhere—everyone was relieved when, after the shock over the present castle owner's death, the young heir took over. Sympathetic feelings toward Viktor rose and so did negative feelings toward Sepp.

Another incident had contributed to Viktor's doubt in Sepp's loyalty. About a year after the unfortunate death of his parents, the banker in Blauenwald, Hermann Reich, had mentioned in a confidential chat with Viktor that Sepp had amassed a substantial amount of money in his account, more than it would be possible from his monthly salary. Sepp was going to be a rich man, if this trend continued and he might be able to buy the castle from Viktor, if he had the power of attorney. Did Viktor then have any idea where Sepp got hold of the money? He did not.

Now the mystery was solved. Sepp had been working on his scheme behind Viktor's and his father's back for many years. And now, in 1985, he was jailed together with the other actual perpetrators. Therefore, when back in 1981 Viktor heard the uncanny demand of his manager, it hit him like a lightning bolt and he decided it was time to leave his childhood behind. He had to put his manager into his place. He learned to make his own decisions regarding Blauenwald.

When he married Betty in California five years after the death of his parents, he was the confirmed master of the estate. And Sepp had been involved in a shady business and was now being tried for being a member of a conspiracy. If convicted, he would have to serve a jail sentence. Paul Sattler was now the manager working under Viktor. The people started to acknowledge the leadership of the new master. But they were still doubtful about his past.

And now there would be the trial starting as soon as January of the new year. Viktor sighed and continued going through his daily correspondence. He picked up the phone and dialed the number of one of the lawyers' offices in nearby Graz. There were no lawyers in Blauenwald.

"Yes, this is Viktor Baumeister from Blauenwald. Could I please speak to *Herrn Dr.* Richter? Well, it's about a personal matter."

A few minutes later Dr. Richter was on the phone. "Yes, *Herr* Baumeister, can I help you?"

"I hope so. Did you hear about the wine tainting scandal that's going on?"

"I read about it in the paper. It's amazing that this had been kept secret for so long. Yes, isn't it your manager, Sepp Wanz, who is involved?"

"Yes, it is. Would you be able to represent him in January?"

After a pause the lawyer answered, "Viktor, if I may call you so, this would not be easy for me. Clearly Sepp has committed a serious crime. However, if you still trust him to continue working for you, I should be able to do something for him. Please allow me some time to find out more about this case and *Herrn* Wanz's motives to join that infamous group of wine tinkers. Things don't look too good for him. I'll get back to you by the end of the month."

So Viktor waited. Meanwhile Dr. Richter contacted the city jail and made an appointment with Sepp for the next day. When the lawyer arrived at the jail, the warden ushered him into a small office and had the prisoner brought in. Sepp had spent a little over a week in jail and had had enough time to think about his sad state of affairs. Not only had his pipe dream about owning the castle some day fallen apart; he also faced a prison sentence. He was in need of legal help and the appearance of a professional lawyer was more than welcome.

Dr. Richter invited Sepp to sit down and relax.

"I am here to defend you, Sepp, if you don't mind my calling you that. Viktor Baumeister contacted me to take up your case. He seems to put great stakes in you in spite of the bad reports. I am considering Viktor's request and might take your case under certain conditions. I do not think that I am able to waive a prison sentence for you at the upcoming trial, but I could ask for reducing the length of time. What's your take on this? Would you cooperate by following the prison rules and being a model inmate?"

It was interesting for the seasoned jurist to watch the expression in Sepp's face, changing slowly from looking sad and apathetic to hopeful and even cheery.

"There was a time," Sepp said almost inaudibly, "when I did not think well of my employer. But that he hired you to defend me is very kind of him. I never thought of Master Viktor as being a kind man. I thought he hated me for wanting to take over his castle. Yes, I will cooperate if this will shorten my sentence." Then he changed his expression again and added accusingly, "Wonder who turned me in. I had everything so well planned."

"As far as I know, one of the other men in your group had turned against you. That happens all the time. There isn't much loyalty among criminals."

"Guess that's what I am now, a criminal!" Sepp said and the glimmer of hope in his face had disappeared. The lawyer began to feel for the man.

"Don't worry, Sepp," he assured him. "I decided to work with you. Yes, Viktor seems to want to keep you. I'll try to do what I can." Dr. Richter got up, shook Sepp's hand and turned to leave. "I'll get in contact with you before the hearing," he told his new client.

Viktor was pleased when the lawyer called him and told him about his decision. He felt that he had made a large step toward taking over the reins of his castle. He still had to fully gain the confidence of his people. The trial dragged on for an entire year.

There was still much left for Betty to do to work on her relationship with her husband. She still did not know Viktor's secret about having seduced the Gypsy girl, Adele. The rumor had not reached her yet.

But first, Viktor would become the father of their child. He was inexperienced about this fact of life and had no idea about what was happening. Betty became pregnant in late August of 1985. The first one to know about her hopeful intuition was her mother. Mary was elated to become a grandmother again. Secretly she wished for a granddaughter. Betty told Viktor after she was almost sure that she was pregnant when she started feeling queasy in the mornings. Late in November she had to vomit right after breakfast and Viktor became concerned. But after she explained to him that this meant they would have a child together, he was overjoyed. His feelings toward this child were very different from the reaction he had felt when Adele had told him about her pregnancy. That time he had felt nothing but displeasure about the inconvenience. Even his confession to the priest, doing penance, and helping the young mother financially, did not ease his distress. He would not have minded if Adele had chosen to have an abortion. But he had not reckoned with Adele's Catholic upbringing. He, Viktor, also was a Catholic, but he was willing to break the rules his church had set. Adele was not. Though he knew that he had fathered a child and that the child was a normal, healthy boy, he had no fatherly feelings for that child. He did not love the mother. Deep down in his subconscious mind he felt guilty and had his friend, the priest, take care of sending money to the mother. But that was all. He tried to forget about the whole thing. Having confessed to Raphael and having absolved penance was enough for his fragile conscience. He was now married to Betty and being able to create a child with her—so it seemed to him—was a sign that God had forgiven his trespasses.

Christmas time was nearing. The entire community was involved in preparations. A huge blue spruce from the castle forest was put up in the *Rittersaal* and children from the village made colorful ornaments for decoration. Viktor told Betty to expect a wonderful festival.

"I know how you celebrate Christmas in America. For most people in your country it is just a big show and they try to display their sentiments on the outside by having the most colorful decorations and giving each other the most lavish gifts. We German speaking people really celebrate the birth of Jesus and in Austria it is the *Kristkindel*, the Christ child that brings peace on earth to the people and gifts to the children. The gift-giving tradition comes from the three Kings from the East who bring their gifts to the new-born King of Heaven and the Peace on Earth is pronounced to the shepherds on the fields by the Angels or the Heavenly Host. It is a quiet, happy occasion, not a noisy and merry one. There will be some dancing in the village, but not too much drinking. You'll hear music everywhere, Christmas songs, concerts, and hymns. Our Raphael will preach a heartwarming sermon and we all will come home from church on Christmas Eve and gather around our tree and distribute presents to our friends from the village and the castle."

"Oh, Viktor, it sounds so wonderful. But, as you know, my parents were brought up in Europe and we never really celebrated with a lot of noise, drinking, and expensive gifts. We didn't even have colored lights outside on our house. My father and mother had a tree, always from our own property at the lake. I was the one in charge of decorating it. And we also sang Christmas songs, many of them German *Lieder.* Mother played the piano and the three of us sang. When I was older, I was allowed to invite friends. Of course, after my marriage to David we always celebrated at the cabin in the mountains together with the parents. Even David's parents joined us sometimes. They, of course, celebrated Hanukkah, and invited my parents to that celebration. I am so thrilled to be part of an Austrian Christmas. Tell me more about what's coming up."

"Well, let's see. Since we now have children in the castle, and even will have one of our very own, we have every reason to celebrate. Usually there was a big tree put up on the *Marktplatz* down in Blauenwald Village, covered with electric lights and ornaments and all the children of the village came, sang Christmas songs, and the mayor's wife distributed presents. The *Buschenschank* had its doors wide open and food and drinks were distributed. We from the castle went down and watched the ceremony. But *Frau* Grete and *Fräulein* Wanz told me that this year they want to celebrate Christmas Eve up here in the castle. Instead of going down to the village, the people with children will come up here and there will be plenty of food, milk, and juices to drink, and presents for the children. I'm told that some children, including your sons, will put on a play. But,"—and Viktor looked a little distressed—"I wasn't supposed to tell you that. Well, forget about it, please."

Betty smiled. "So, that's why I wasn't supposed to ask questions when the boys asked me for money to buy material for costumes."

"I guess. They all want to surprise you. I hope I didn't spoil it for you."

"Oh, Viktor, now I'm really looking forward to Christmas. And, come to think of it, next Christmas there will be three children!"

"Betty, we have a lot to be thankful for. I hope 'it' looks like you."

"I'd rather 'it' looks like you." Betty looked fondly at her handsome husband.

Christmas came and went. It was a lovely event. The staff outdid itself. The castle was turned upside down, everything was cleaned and polished. The rooms were decorated with fresh branches from the forest and presents piled up around the tree. The villagers came up to the castle, greeted the new mistress, wished her luck, and gave advice for the expected baby—no big secret anymore—though she did not need much of that. After all, she had produced two great boys. Secretly she wished for a girl.

The children's play was a great success. Several girls and boys from the village had joined Nathan and Jacob and with Nathan's teacher's help they presented the nativity scene in a three-act play.

In January the trial of the wine tainters took place and, as predicted, all five of them were found guilty. While four of them received life sentences, Sepp only had to serve four years in prison. Since the trial proceedings had dragged on over a year's time, Sepp started serving his sentence at the state penitentiary at the beginning of 1987 and would be released in 1991. Dr. Richter had been able to plead for the reduction of a much longer sentence. The people in the castle felt relieved. After all, Sepp had been a good manager.

Betty took good care of herself and followed Dr. Amato's advice to take it easy. She felt good and people around her noticed that she was blossoming and radiating happiness. Gerda was at her beck and call all the time. For her, Betty's pregnancy was almost like expecting her own baby.

The time of delivery drew near. Dr. Amato had told the Baumeisters that the baby would be due around May 25. "It could be a few days earlier or later. Just be prepared and don't do much strenuous work, *Frau* Baumeister." He shook hands with them and left for another patient.

Dr. Amato had come to Blauenwald a few years after the priest Raphael, during 1974. His parents had come from Japan after the end of World War II, and had settled in Germany, where their son was born, but then had moved to Austria during the 1960s because they liked the climate better in the more southern country. Their son had been a good student in school and after graduating from high school was sent to Vienna to study medicine. He passed his necessary exams, but could not find a place at a good hospital in Austria's capital. He sent out applications, was rejected, and decided to start his own practice in Blauenwald where the elderly Dr. Hollmann had decided to retire and had put his practice up for sale. Dr. Amato had asked Hermann Reich for a loan, had qualified for it, and had settled in Blauenwald. He was successful and his practice grew. After a while he could afford to hire an assistant and *Fräulein* Frieda accepted the job. They lived together in an apartment above his practice in the center of town and even became lovers. He proved to be a good doctor, cured many colds, did a variety of operations, and helped several young Blauenwald villagers to be born. One of his first cases had been the young Gypsy girl Adele. He had confirmed her pregnancy and had given her good advice to take care of herself.

However, in spite of his success Dr. Amato was not an entirely happy man. Being an Oriental and an outsider of the closely knit little village, he felt that he needed to be more accepted and tried to achieve this by being overly friendly and familiar with the people. He even gave in to breaking his *Oath to Hippocrates*; at least the part of swearing to "hold his patients conditions to himself." Therefore he was partially responsible for rumors spreading in Blauenwald. Young Adele was not the only person whose privacy was invaded. He also had contributed to revealing Sepp Wanz's shady operations. With other words, Dr. Amato was a gossip and Frieda was no purist either.

There was no other doctor around in Blauenwald. When Betty's labor pains started in the evening, it was Dr. Amato who came to deliver the baby. They depended on him to do a good job.

It was assumed by many people that this child was Viktor's first. He had never attended a birth and he was excited. He had no idea what was in store for him. On the evening of May 23 Betty started labor. It felt different from the times she had her boys and she was almost certain that it was a girl this time.

"Better be ready, Viktor. Please call Dr. Amato now," she told her husband. They had decided to have the baby in the castle. One of the guest rooms had been prepared with sheets, towels, an electric plate to boil water, and all the paraphernalia necessary to help the little newcomer enter the world. *Frau* Grete had helped to deliver Viktor, so she had some experience in birthing. She herself, though, never had children of her own. Gerda, on the other hand, had never been present when a human was born. Her only acquaintance with birthing was with animals. She anticipated the worst. She promised Betty to sit by her and hold her hand through the ordeal. It was a long night and Betty had to gather all her strength to stifle her urge to cry out. Viktor went back and forth, wringing his hands. It was hot; everyone was suffocating.

"Do all women suffer this much?" he asked Dr. Amato who watched Betty closely.

"This is a very normal birth," was the laconic answer. The labor pains had started in the evening at eight o'clock and at six in the morning Elisabeth Marie Baumeister was born and presented to the proud parents. Frieda, Dr. Amato's assistant, had caught the strapping baby, had washed her, and expertly bundled her up in soft cloth diapers.

Everybody was happy that Betty had finally done it and could rest now peacefully. Viktor took her in his arms and felt like a newborn being also. Secretly he wondered if Adele had suffered like this and for the first time in ten years he felt pangs of remorse. What a magical occurrence is the birth of a baby! They had chosen to spell the baby's name the German way, since the little girl would stay in a German speaking country. Mary Fromm, the proud grandmother, was happy to see her granddaughter carrying her original name, Marie. Later on, though, the little girl would become a simple "Liesl."

And hardly anyone knew for sure that Liesl had a biological brother.

CHAPTER 6

Adele

Adele Boraq, the Gypsy girl who was so unfairly raped by Viktor when only fourteen, had gone back to her family in 1975 and lived with them in Gypsytown, a suburb of Pristina, a formidable city, capital of Kosovo. Her parents had died long ago, killed by fanatic soldiers of the Kosovo Liberation Army, consisting mostly of Muslim Albanians. Her relatives lived in crowded quarters and when the baby, a beautiful, spirited boy, was born, the situation became even tighter. When, in addition to deprivation in the too small apartment, political fights broke out between Albanian Muslim "freedom fighters" and Serbian Catholic Christians, Adele's tribe had to endure bitter hardship.

Researchers have found—in contrast to some people's opinions that their name might suggest they came from Egypt—that the Gypsies had come to Europe from Asia during the ninth century. Because of their nomadic lifestyle they were highly misunderstood and looked down upon by many, more sedative citizens. Gypsies are also referred to as Romas or Romanies. Adele's tribe was less inclined to move around than other Romas. They had been satisfied staying in the city of Pristina as long as Tito, the stern president of Yugoslavia, ruled the country. But Tito died in 1980 and the status of Kosovo within the multi-ethnic union of the Baltic States began to crumble. Albanian rebels formed a guerilla army and proceeded to oust Serbs and Montenegrins. Rather than packing up and wandering away from Pristina, they only moved a few miles to a village called Pristina Polje where they erected a tent city and stayed behind barricades. Here they felt safer and also had a small church and village school near-by.

Adele, who had secretly hoped that Viktor might change his mind and marry her, sadly acknowledged the fact that this would never happen. She could not agree to an abortion, though this would have been legal in Austria at that time. She was a good Catholic and knew that it was God's will to keep her baby. Her relatives accepted her reluctantly and she managed to raise her boy as well as she could. She even afforded an education at the village school by selling home-made crafts and dancing and singing performances for the villagers. She named the boy August, after her late father.

August was four years old when they moved to Pristina Polje. Adele became very religious. Most of the Romas were Catholics and the orphaned young mother found a friendly priest to look after her and her son. Raphael from Blauenwald managed to get in contact with this priest. He sent him the money that Viktor gave him monthly to send to Adele for her upkeep. That was the only thing Viktor did to redeem the terrible wrong he had done to Adele and their son. The other Romas thought that Adele was able to raise her son by herself. They never knew about August's father and his contributions. Her family had no inkling of the existence of Viktor Baumeister and the Blauenwald estate. Adele kept this strictly to herself. She never was too intimate with her family.

The boy stayed close to his mother who was not very strong and needed him very much. He was everything to her and she to him. The other boys his age teased him and called him "Mommy boy" but August did not care. He felt proud to take care of his pretty mother.

When August was eight years old, his mother insisted that he go to school. He was an intelligent lad and she had taught him whatever she knew. She could read a little and had August practice his letters, words, and simple sentences. When he went to school in Kosovo Polje for the first time, he noticed that the other boys were reading books. He knew he had to catch up and improved his literary skills with amazing speed. Every day when he came home from school, he had learned new skills. After one year the teacher visited his mother and told her that her boy was very gifted and that he was very pleased having him in his class. August was not only intelligent, he was handsome. He had inherited his father's muscular build and his mother's raven beauty. He also displayed a musical talent. But he was completely oblivious to these attributes and was neither vain nor conceited. He did not think much about the future. One thing, though, worried him. The other children in the tribe had fathers and mothers. He only had a mother. Sometimes, when he was in a gloomy mood, he approached his mother with questions, which she avoided answering.

"Mother, where is my father? Who is he? Why don't we ever see him?"

"Your father is a wonderful man, but he abandoned us. That's all you ought to know, son." Adele said this so emphatically that August felt that it was useless to ask any more questions. But he was moody after such fruitless talks. In his dreams his father came to him, a beautiful, tall man who talked to him in a friendly way. When he reached out to embrace him, his father vanished and August woke up, bathed in sweat. He developed a feeling of hatred toward this man whom he was supposed to love. What the boy did not know was that his father partly supported them. Adele kept the regular money contributions that she received via the church a deep secret. Nobody was supposed to know about that. Everybody thought that Adele earned the money for their living all by herself.

However—the harsh life did not agree with her—she contracted pneumonia and became severely ill. The village priest, in contact with Raphael in Blauenwald, became concerned and visited the sick woman often. And so, life went on until August was eleven years old.

Viktor never inquired about Adele and her child. His conscience was satisfied by giving money to Raphael to take care of the problem. He shifted his own problem to someone else. He let the priest handle it. His sin lay deeply buried in his subconscious.

BOOK TWO

1987

CHAPTER 7

Brenner's Visit

Letter from Kathryn Carlton to Jacob Goldstein.

Oakland, May 3rd, 1987
My dearest Jacob. I am so happy. Dad and Mom decided
to let me visit you in July. Grandpa and Grandma are going
and want me to go too. I can hardly wait to see all of you
again, especially you. Do you still speak English? Grandma
Erma wants us all to learn German. Aunt Lotti and Uncle
Peter are coming too. Mom helped me with this letter.
Love you, Kathryn.

It was the middle of July in 1987. Back in the castle preparations
were in the making for the visit of the Brenners from California. It
was just a few days until school would be out, and the boys had a
great summer to look forward to. And the day after tomorrow Viktor's relatives from California would arrive! The boys remembered
the Brenners well and they looked forward to seeing little Kathryn
Carlton again. However, the other Carltons, the parents Heidi and
Richard, could not afford to make the big trip just now. Heidi, like
Betty, had a brand-new baby girl named Gretchen in 1986 and had
her hands full. They would come later, when everything was more
settled. But they let Kathryn go with her grandparents, Hans and
Erma Brenner, because it would be a wonderful experience for her
and she would see her good friends Nathan and Jacob again. Kathryn had promised her parents to be extra good and she had kept this
promise.

It was Sunday afternoon and the boys had found a nice, green spot close to the stables to sit down. They were talking about the visitors from California.

"I'm so happy that they are coming Wednesday," said Jacob. "Did you know that Kathryn is coming with them?" Jacob pulled the little pink envelope out of his pocket and showed Nathan the letter.

Nathan was impressed. "Wow, she wrote that? But she is not even six years old. She just started school."

"She wrote that her mother helped her."

"Okay, makes sense. Isn't her mother a schoolteacher?"

"Yes. We'll have fun with Kathryn. She's such a good sport."

"She's okay. She's always so happy. And she loves to sing." Nathan remembered when the Carltons had come to one of the storytelling meetings at his grandmother's cabin. The Fromms had a piano at their cabin and his grandmother Mary had shown him how to find chords and scales and to put melodies together from memory. Little Kathryn, then only three, had loved to listen and sing songs that Nathan was soon able to pick up. The two had spent many happy hours making music together.

"And she loves to run around and investigate things."

"Like the time she almost drowned and you rescued her."

"Well, I just saw her in the lake and screamed. Her father jumped in the water and caught her. And Aunt Lotti gave her mouth-to-mouth …"

"… Resuscitation. Right, but if you hadn't seen her in the water …" Nathan paused. "So, you will always be her hero."

Both boys smiled at each other.

Jacob picked up the conversation again. "Aren't you glad that school's over for today? And Wednesday is the last day, just in time for the Brenners' visit. Any homework for you?" Jacob asked his older brother.

"Not much, just that essay about the unrest in Bosnia and Kosovo. But guess what, Jacob; I'm taking music lessons at the beginning of the next term. They asked us what instrument we would like to play. I chose the violin."

"That's nice, Nathan. I wouldn't care for that so much. All that practicing. But then, I'm just not good at music. I'm tone-deaf. I'd rather take lessons in agriculture, things you have to know when you become a manager like Mr. Wanz."

"Yes, you always like to be outside. I don't like to ruin my hands. I won't mind the practicing, in fact, I'd love it. I'd like to become a famous violinist."

"That won't be so easy, but I know, you always like to be by yourself, reading books and doing your homework. No wonder you are such a model student. I just can't sit still. I have to do things."

While the brothers were talking, the sun had gone down and Nathan looked at his watch. "It's close to supper time; let's go in before they look for us. I don't want to cause trouble."

"Right, you're always so proper. Besides, I'm rather hungry. Hope *Frau* Schwarz has made my favorite, *Zwetschgenknödel.*" (dumplings filled with stewed prunes)

"I don't like *Knödel* that much. Remember our old home? Mom always had special foods for us on Friday evenings. That's when *Shabbat* begins. And on Saturdays we didn't have school."

"Right, here we have to slave even on Saturday. But this Saturday it's already vacation and Viktor will take all of us to Vienna. And the Brenners too. I am looking forward to that."

"Me too, especially to the opera at night. We'll see *Don Giovanni,* remember? I love Mozart. I'm going to play his music. Aren't you looking forward to Saturday?"

"Sure, mostly to see the river and to eat at the Sacher Café. I might fall asleep during the opera."

"Oh you, always thinking of food. But yes, I hear they have live music at the Sacher Café. I'd love to hear the *Blue Danube Waltz.* Viktor lets me play the piano in the library. Grandma Mary will give me lessons. Mom found some old music books that belong to Viktor. It's really easy to play piano. Violin will be harder. Maybe Kathryn will sing with us. She has such a pretty voice."

While thus talking about the visitors and the planned trip to Vienna, the boys had reached the castle gate and went up the stairway to the second floor. They met their mother who indeed had become worried and was relieved to see her sons. "There you two are. Quick, get ready for supper; don't make us wait for you." With a look at Jacob she added, "*Frau* Schwarz has prepared your favorite tonight, Jacob, *Zwetschgenknödel.*"

"Swell, we'll be right there." The boys went to their room, did a brief washing to get rid of the stable odors, slipped on fresh shirts, and made it just in time to get into their seats before Hanni came with the piping hot platter full of good food to serve the hungry people.

"Tell me, Nathan," asked Viktor, "did you have a chance to look over the article on *Don Giovanni* so you will be able to follow the plot and won't fall asleep on Saturday night?"

"I certainly did, Viktor. I can hardly wait for Saturday."

Both boys preferred to call their new stepfather by his first name and Viktor understood. Nathan especially had a hard time adjusting to his father's death and nobody, not even Viktor, could replace his real father. Betty had tried to instill the due respect they owed their new father in the boys and Jacob had no issue addressing him as "Father." But Nathan was different. He resented having to change to Catholicism and silently clung to his Jewish upbringing. The only thing he really embraced in his new home was the love of music in Austria. Here he could enjoy listening to music whenever he wanted to. In singing activities at school Nathan's natural musical talent was soon discovered by his teachers. Not only was his voice leading in the acappella choir—he also excelled in everything else related to music. He was highly recommended for free music lessons—taught by a special teacher from Graz—and made remarkable progress in a short time. Betty's mother Mary played the piano well and had even been asked to play the organ during services at church. Nathan must have inherited his love of music from her. She was proud to contribute thus to the beauty of the church service. His father David had always fostered musical education for the boys, though Jacob did not prove to be talented and had preferred more practical subjects, and above all, sports.

Viktor and Betty were overjoyed about the Brenners' decision to accept their invitation in the summer of 1987, when both Hans and

Erma Brenner, two of their children, Lotti and Peter, and their oldest granddaughter would have a six-week vacation during the summer months. Three weeks would be spent at the castle in Austria, the remaining three weeks in Germany. Erma Brenner did all the planning and preparation; and a good planner she was!

Summer arrived faster than anybody thought and before long five members of the Brenner family in California were ready for the big trip to Europe. They were Hans and Erma, both retired from their respective jobs, Lotti, a twenty-seven year-old nurse, Peter, twenty, a sophomore in college, and six year-old Kathryn. They planned to stay from the middle of July through the end of August. George Updike, Lotti's husband since the big Lake Dweller wedding party in 1985, had to stay in California because of his work as a swimming instructor and also to take care of their mountain house. Lotti had gotten six weeks off from her job. Heidi, the Brenners' oldest, and husband Rich, both school teachers, had decided to come during their summer vacation in a few years.

Luise Gilmann, the Brenners' neighbor in Oakland, living with her grandmother Anna, would be driving the four Brenners and Kathryn to the airport in San Francisco. It would be the first time for the middle-aged couple to leave their home after being married for almost thirty-five years. Lotti had come down from Springlake the night before the departure in her little Karman Ghia, packed and ready to go. Kathryn also had spent the night with her grandparents. After all the people and luggage were stashed away in Hans's big station wagon and Luise sat ready at the wheel, her grandmother, Anna Gilmann, came over with some provisions for the trip: sandwiches, cookies, even a few bottles of Snapple. All of that was packed neatly into a small rucksack, which would be handy for daytrips in Austria. She handed this welcomed gift through the window and everybody thanked her for her warm heart.

"Anna, how nice of you. Now we certainly won't forget you whenever we hike in Austria. And something to eat between airplane meals." Erma leaned out of the car window and shook Anna's hand.

"That's okay, Erma. Just have a safe flight and come back in one piece. Luise and I will miss you."

"Let's go, folks," said Luise who did not want her neighbors to miss their plane. Erma closed the window. All the Brenners waved to Anna who went back to her house slowly. She and Luise would miss their good neighbors this summer.

The ride to the airport, through the city of Oakland, across the Bay Bridge, and south on Highway 101, took less than an hour. The weather was clear, the temperature pleasantly cool, and the Brenners looked forward to their first flight to another continent.

"Look at that plane, it just took off. In a short while it's us who are sitting in one of those." Peter was very excited. Most of his college friends had been to Europe, or at least out of California. Almost all of them had flown. For him it was the first time. He pinched Lotti to get her attention. Lotti was excited too, but she had already been around the airport. George and she had flown to Banff in Canada, where they had friends. George had met Christopher at the ski resort in the Sierra, where both of them were working as ski instructors. George had invited Christopher to his cabin and then accepted an invitation to Banff, Christopher's hometown in the Cascades. They had even rented a cabin on the shore of Lake Louise for their honeymoon.

The Brenners found their seats on the huge jet plane to Frankfurt, Germany, from where they would change to another plane. They enjoyed every second of the take-off above beautiful San Francisco, up, up, up, into the blue yonder. Soon they were above the morning clouds and relaxed. Erma took out a novel, Hans a newspaper, Lotti a medical journal, and Peter a Rubik's Cube. Kathryn had chosen her favorite teddy bear and had plenty of coloring books and crayons in her backpack. Peter fiddled with the radio in the armrest of his seat and put on his listening device. He helped the others to do the same thing. The friendly stewardess came by and offered various drinks. The Brenners were looking forward to a long flight, first to Frankfurt in Germany, then a connecting flight to Vienna.

In Vienna they took a train to Graz and from there a bus to their final destination, Leibnitz in southern Styria. There Viktor picked them up to bring them to Blauenwald Castle, where they would stay for three wonderful weeks. Betty had decided to stay home with the baby and the boys were in school, so it was just he, standing in front of the depot, when the bus from Graz rolled in. The Brenners recognized the tall man in his Austrian clothes, just as they remembered him from two years ago in California.

"There is Viktor. He hasn't changed a bit!" Peter shouted, very excited.

They all scrambled out of the bus and surrounded Viktor who beamed happily.

"Welcome to Austria, you all look great," he greeted them, trying to shake ten hands at the same time. He picked up Kathryn and swung her high up in the air with his strong arms. "You have grown a foot since I saw you last!" he said after he had put her down gently. Kathryn, who reached to his belt now, put her little arms around his legs and squeezed him hard. She loved her "Uncle" Viktor. He and the bus driver took the luggage out from the storage compartment under the bus and carried it over to the Baumeisters' big station wagon.

They all piled in and Viktor drove them through the rolling hills of southern Styria. Soon the castle came into view, sitting majestically on top of Castle Hill. Up, up, up went the road, past Sepp Wanz's little house, through the linden alley, past the stables and into the courtyard where Betty was waiting with little Baby Liesl in her arms, flanked by *Fräulein* Gerda and *Frau* Grete. They had arrived at the castle, finally, after so many hours of traveling!

It was a weekday and most of the staff was hard at work. After the welcome ceremony, after having settled in their rooms, and after the dust from traveling was washed away, the family met on the verandah where *Frau* Grete's helpers served a wonderful *Jause*. Peter (Peter Brenner's namesake), the German shepherd—a descendent from Rudolf's dog Prinz—went from one to the other, wagging his tail welcoming the guests.

Viktor told them that nothing was planned for the next few days, but on Saturday they all would go to Vienna, take a tour of the city, and see an opera at night.

"But first you have to get used to our beautiful country. I want you all to feel at home in our castle. You are free to do whatever you want. We will take all our meals together and I hope that you like our food. Soon the boys will be home from school. They are so excited to meet you all…again."

Just as he said this, they heard a loud *Hallo* and in stormed the two Goldstein boys, just as the Brenners remembered them, only several inches taller. Nathan was now almost Viktor's size, Jacob about a head shorter. "Last day of school, thank God." They all embraced.

"Shall we speak English or German?" asked Lotti whose German was not too hot.

"Just talk as you like, most all of us are bilingual," said Betty, realizing that Peter and Lotti only had scant knowledge of conversational German after the few courses of formal study in that language in school. "After you have stayed with us for a few weeks, you'll be fluent in German, all of you, I promise. Look at me. I am a living example."

"But you are so good at languages," Peter said. "I know you and Viktor spoke German together at the wedding."

"How observant, Peter. It was I who taught her." Viktor proudly mentioned. Betty smiled. She had learned German in school and college. But Viktor deserved some credit, he spoke to her in his native Austrian accent and Betty was a good student.

Erma spoke up. "Peter and Lotti, you should be ashamed. We *always* encouraged you children to speak German with us. And you had German classes at school. So I propose that we speak German like everybody else here."

"Oh Mom, that's easy for you to say."

"If you want to be in good standing with all the folks around the castle and the village, you better learn to speak German," was Grandpa Luther's advice.

Grandma Mary just beamed happily and looked at all the familiar faces. "It doesn't matter to me at all what language you speak. It's so wonderful to have you all with us."

"Let's drink to that and *willkommen* to our castle!" All followed Viktor's friendly advice and lifted their glasses of *Heuringer* (bottled house wine) that the ever caring *Frau* Grete had put in front of everybody. The young boys and Kathryn, of course, had fruit juice. A noisy clicking of glasses took place.

A lively chat about their trip evolved and finally the guests excused themselves and went to their rooms.

Peter, the budding history student, was very interested in everything about the castle and before retiring had asked Viktor to lend him some literature about the history of Blauenwald. He had learned some general facts about European history in high school and was well aware of facts leading up to the unrest in the Baltic States. He realized that the castle was situated at the crossroad used by migrating nations long ago and that its history was closely related to the complicated past of the Austrian-Hungarian empire.

It was after midnight when Peter put down the report. Tomorrow he would learn more about those ancestors of Viktor. He intended to have a good talk with *Frau* Grete who, as he had heard, had been with the Baumeisters longer than anyone else at the castle. But then he remembered that *Frau* Grete did not speak English. In fact, the German spoken by all the people here was very unlike the High German he had been learning in high school. He had no trouble *reading* the language, but understanding the Austrian accent was a different thing. He decided that it would be better to use the first few days to mingle with his relatives whose German was less accented and to wait before asking the natives too many questions. After all, they would not even be able to understand him!

After promising himself not to speak a single word of English from now on, he turned out the light and went to sleep.

CHAPTER 8

Vienna

After a few days of acclimatizing, the Brenners were ready for the big outing to Vienna. It was amazing how fast everyone had learned to communicate in German. Peter's resolve to immerse himself in the language had helped them all.

On Saturday morning the Brenner family with Kathryn, Betty's two boys, and Viktor left early in the comfortable family wagon. Betty and the Fromm parents had decided to stay at the castle with little Liesl. The trip took them through the rolling hills of northern Styria into the extensive basin of Vienna. The province of Vienna, which has the city of Vienna as its capital, is the largest region of the Republic of Austria. It's also called "Lower Austria" because it is basically flat land without mountains.

They arrived in Vienna around ten o'clock. After parking the car, they first walked on Ringstraße, and marveled at the facades of the colossal Staatsoper and the half circular Hofburg, which used to be the residence of the empress of Austria-Hungary, Elisabeth, the frivolous wife of Emperor Franz Josef, known as "Sisi," and memorialized in several movies. When they reached the Museum of Fine Arts, and had their fill of Rubens, Rembrandt, Dürer, and Brueghel, they felt ready for a meal. Viktor had planned for this and had reserved a table at the renowned Sacher Café in walking distance from the Ringstraße, where they had an authentic Wiener Schnitzel and a slice of the famous Sacher Torte for dessert. Jacob and Kathryn loved everything, Nathan just nibbled at some of the unfamiliar delicacies. "I'm ready for a nap," was all Hans could say after the last bite of this overly rich concoction.

"Right, so let's walk down to the river and sit down on a bench next to the Danube, with a view of the *Donauturm*."

"That looks just like the Seattle Space needle. Can't be hundreds of years old as the other things we already saw," was Peter's remark, when they had reached the bank of the river and had settled down comfortably on a pretty green bench.

"Let's sit here and rest for at least half an hour," proposed Viktor. "Then we'll visit the *Hofburg* and after that it's almost time to get ready for the opera."

"What opera are we going to see?" Erma wanted to know.

"It's *Don Giovanni*, Mozart's finest opera, full of suspense, humor, and good music." Viktor explained. "You'll feel good afterwards; the bad guy is burned up and goes to hell for all his bad deeds."

"That's as it should be," practical Lotti opined. She was such a fine young lady, always cheerful, always agreeable, always a joy to be with. She radiated happiness wherever she went. Peter was different. He liked to act knowledgeably, loved attention, and acted sometimes a little smart-alecky. He was a handsome young man, but did not have many friends. Especially girls, attracted by his good looks, found him boring after a while because he always seemed to know everything and made them feel that they could not live up to his high standards. Kathryn was everyone's friend. She was outgoing, full of life, and always ready to learn new things. She and Jacob were inseparable.

They easily found their way back to the *Hofburg* in the center of Vienna. This classical residence castle is still inhabited by Austrian federal presidency. Of course, they couldn't possibly see the entire sprawling palace—it was much too big. So Viktor had selected one part that all of them would enjoy: the *Schatzkammer*, which includes the crown of the Holy Roman Empire and many other treasures and the *Nationalbibliothek Prunksaal*—the peak of Baroque architecture designed by Johann Fischer von Erlach and built by his son. Here Peter was in his element. He had studied European history at college and almost knew more than their guide told them in his halting English. Peter also informed the group about the famous Spanish Riding School with its Lipizzaner stallions, which were housed in this palace. He had prepared himself by going to the library and reading up on books about Austria. All this knowledge was not going to waste.

"Can't we see the White Lipizzaners? I know they train them here in the *Hofburg.*"

Viktor smiled. "Well, Peter, you should be the guide around here. I would love to see those horses too. Maybe we have to come back to Vienna. I did not reserve tickets for that event for today. That's so famous that you have to call in at least a year before you want to see it. It's always sold out. So are events featuring the Vienna Choir Boys. You just can't see everything in one day. Maybe you should come back to us some day and you and I'll go see those horses together."

"Swell, Viktor. It's a deal." Peter loved his cousin.

Viktor had purchased tickets for the *Wiener Staatsoper.* This impressive neo-romantic building, almost as big as a city block, was a sight by itself. When the family had checked their coats and mounted the stairs to the first floor where they found their seats in the huge interior with blazing lights and the hum of about two thousand voices, they were overwhelmed. "Viktor, this is fabulous," was all Erma could say.

"How old is this building?" Peter wanted to know.

"As far as I know, the original Vienna Court Opera had been inaugurated in 1869, but was partly destroyed during World War II by Allied bombs. Only the foyer and the main stairways, the vestibule, and the tearoom were spared. But the rest, including décor and props for more than one hundred twenty operas, was gone. It had been renamed Vienna State Opera in 1920. By 1955 the rebuilt house was reopened and you can see that they did a good job. It now seats 2,200 persons. It looks like it's sold out tonight."

"Where did the people go to see great opera in the meantime?" Lotti wanted to know.

"I can't really answer that," replied Viktor. "I guess they had performances at the *Volksoper* (people's opera) or in other cities, like Salzburg or Graz. People in Austria cannot live without their visits to the opera. Music education is stressed from early on. I was not even born until after the end of World War II, but I do remember my parents taking me to Vienna's People's Opera several times a year. There we saw famous operettas like *Sound of Music* or *The Gypsies' Baron.* Once they put on Puccini's *La Bohéme* in Graz, in the *Grazer Opernhaus,* which is not so shabby, either. The first time I went to see *Fidelio* by Beethoven in the newly reconstructed Vienna Opera, I was so amazed. Just like you people now."

The tickets Viktor had bought were seats close to the center in the third row of the first floor. He had splurged. Those tickets were not cheap. When it was eight o'clock and the orchestra, that had been busy tuning instruments, quieted, and the conductor, Claudio Abbado, lifted his baton to start the powerful overture, all talking ceased—it became so quiet; one could hear a pin drop. The overture commenced and for fifteen minutes people listened spellbound. When the heavy brocade curtain opened and the first act began, showing Leporello waiting for his master who is courting Donna Anna and complaining about his pitiful job, followed by the immediate action of Don Giovanni killing the powerful Sevillian lady's father, the audience relaxed and followed the drama, listening to the beautiful music.

The Brenners had been, under the tutelage of Viktor, carefully prepared for seeing this particular opera, and they followed the two long acts attentively. Though San Francisco features a formidable opera house, the Brenners had not experienced many visits to see operas. They were busy during the week and needed the weekends for relaxation or going to their cabin. When at the end of Act Two Giovanni was engulfed in fire, Peter sighed with relief. "He had it coming." Nathan was enraptured and did not lose a beat of the music. When Erma looked at the two younger children, she saw that they tried hard to keep awake and follow the performance, especially Jacob. Kathryn was soon fast asleep with her head in Lotti's lap. Erma smiled. No wonder, the six-year-old was exhausted. She had been on the go all day long. And Jacob? He had told her that he might fall asleep. Opera just wasn't his favorite thing. But he was fascinated by the plot and the dashing character of the Don.

Nathan loved every second of the grand opera. He had studied the libretto diligently and had practiced most of the beautiful arias on the piano at the castle.

The family left with the crowd, slowly walking down the carpeted stairs, enjoying the foyer with frescoes by Moritz von Schwind, and stepping in to the brightly lit street.

It was close to midnight and after loading his guests into the station wagon, Viktor brought his family home. While driving through the country, now dark, the three young men in the back seat were discussing the events of the day, especially the opera.

"Peter, you have seen operas before in San Francisco. How did that compare with what we saw tonight?" Nathan wanted to know.

"My experience with opera is not so great; I only saw the *Zauberflöte* by Mozart and liked it fine. My parents are too busy to take us out very often. Jacob, what did you think of that scoundrel Giovanni?"

"I hated him. I was glad he burned in the fire. But I could have understood the words better without all that music."

"Now that's ridiculous, Jacob. The whole purpose of the opera is the music and the singing. Without music it would be a drama." Nathan shook his head over the ignorance of his brother.

"Which means that I like a drama better than an opera. What do you think, Peter?"

"Maybe I agree with you, Jacob. But I also loved the music tonight. So I must agree with Nathan too."

After some thinking Jacob asked the two others, "Do you think that the Don would have come to his senses even without the old general interfering? Maybe he wasn't such a bad man at all. Remember how Leporello really liked him. Maybe he shouldn't have burned."

"Oh, Jacob, don't worry about all that. Who cares? That part is important to the opera. Giovanni was evil and had to be destroyed. Otherwise the opera wouldn't end the way it did. And didn't you love the great ending? That bad man suffering in the fire?"

"Oh yes, but I wonder how they did that."

"Did what?"

"The fire."

Here Peter intervened. "That wasn't a real fire, Jacob. They used some chemicals that made it look like a fire. We studied that in chemistry. I must agree; they did a marvelous job."

Just then the wagon rolled over the loose gravel of the parking garage and they were back at the castle.

* * *

Not until 1987 when the Brenners from California visited, and not since 1985 when life at the castle had changed drastically for all inhabitants, were foreboding signals from the attic picked up again by *Frau* Grete. Before the next life-changing event happened during the summer months, the Baumeisters and Fromms had been looking forward to the visit of their relatives and friends from Oakland, California. On Saturday morning, after her family and friends had left for Vienna, Betty visited the kitchen to talk to *Frau* Grete about the menus for the following week. She found the cook sitting at one of the preparation tables, flanked by Erika and Hanni, two of the helpers, who stared at her open-mouthed.

"You don't say, *Frau* Schwarz, you heard that noise again? Did it wake you up in the middle of the night?"

"Well, as I keep telling you, the *Spuk* is getting at it again. This night I could hardly sleep."

"What did you hear this time?" Erika asked.

"Oh, this time they were really loud. There was a noise like running around and stomping and also as if they were fighting."

"Aren't you scared, *Frau* Schwarz?"

"I'm scared that something bad will happen. Hope not an accident or something like that."

"Did your husband hear it too, *Frau* Schwarz?" Hanni wanted to know.

"Oh him, he doesn't hear much anymore. He slept through all that ruckus."

Betty had entered the kitchen and listened to the conversation. "I'm sorry that you didn't sleep well, *Frau* Schwarz," she said.

"Maybe we should look into the cause of that noise. How long has it been since someone has been up in the attic?"

"Oh, no, *Gnädige Frau,* they wouldn't like that. They just want me to know something is happening."

"If you say so, *Frau* Schwarz," Betty said, dismissing the case with a shrug of her shoulders. "I came to ask about your plans for the coming week."

Soon *Frau* Grete was concentrating on the menu and forgetting her forebodings. The girls went back to their work and Betty returned to the upper floor to care for her baby. Though she had not shown it, she was a little disturbed by *Frau* Grete's talking. Maybe something was happening? But then she checked herself. She was not used to being without her family at the castle and she should not brood. No reason for that. On the way up the stairs she met Gerda, looking happy and busy as always.

"Good morning," and turning her head around to see if anyone was near, she added "Betty."

"Good morning, Gerda. I just come up from the kitchen."

"Oh, oh, that's why you are looking a little glum. *Frau* Grete's at it again with the *Spuk*?" Gerda looked concerned. "I talked to her earlier. She couldn't sleep last night. But don't let that bother you. I didn't hear a thing."

"That's because you are young and still sleep all night," Betty said, smiling. "Some day I should tell my husband about this noise in the attic—if it isn't mostly *Frau* Grete's imagination. But he has other things on his mind. And now we have guests."

And so, the *Spuk* was soon forgotten, though it left Betty a little worried. She was not used to being by herself all day long. She told Gerda that she would take her meals with her parents in their apartment, so it would be easier for everyone.

Mary and Luther were happy to have Betty and the baby with them and they spent a nice afternoon together.

After the evening meal, which Gerda delivered personally to the Fromms apartment, Betty and her parents settled in the sitting room to wait for their family and guests to come home.

"When do you expect them to get back?" Mary asked Betty.

"Around eleven, or so. Maybe later. I don't know how long the opera will take. It could be as late as midnight."

Betty had been waiting for them since after the evening meal. The baby had been crying for a while and Mary and Betty had taken turns walking slowly up and down with her until she finally fell asleep. Peter, the German shepherd, had settled at Betty's feet and was dozing comfortably. Luther had already gone to bed early and Mary followed him when the party hadn't returned by ten o'clock. So Betty and the dog were by themselves when the phone rang around eleven o'clock. Peter, the dog, sat up and started growling. Something unexpected must have happened. Betty picked up the phone—it was the guard from the gate.

"Good evening, Ma'am, this is Rupert. Sorry to disturb you so late. There is a young man here, and he insists on speaking to the master of the castle. I told him that the master is not in and he still insists he has to talk to someone. Would you let him come up?"

"Sure, Rupert, send him up. Who could that be, so late in the evening? Tell the young man that I am in the sitting room."

"Yes. He looks like he needs help. I'll send him up. Let me know if you need me. Good night, *Frau* Baumeister."

Betty was glad she hadn't undressed yet. She waited for the unexpected guest. After a little while she heard someone coming up the stairs and then timidly knocking on the door. She shushed the growling dog before he started to bark.

"Come in, it's open," she called. The door opened slowly and in came a boy, much like her Nathan, maybe a little younger, extremely good-looking, but a little hunch-backed. He would be of Nathan's height, if he straightened up. His clothes were rags, as if he had just come from a long, adventurous journey. He stood there, cap in hand, saying barely audible, "I want to see my father."

"And who'd that be," asked Betty, puzzled.

"Viktor Baumeister, Ma'am."

Betty was speechless. Her head was spinning. After a while during which both had stared at each other, Betty asked, "What is your name, please?"

"I am August," he said. Betty could hardly hear him.

"And you are Viktor's son?"

"Yes, Ma'am. Nobody here knows me. My mother just died yesterday and I have no place to go but to my father." … "She wanted me to," he added after a while.

Betty had gathered her courage. "August, let me introduce myself. I am *Frau* Baumeister, Betty, married to Viktor since 1985. Did you know that your father had married …?" And she added slowly … "again?"

"Yes, Ma'am, my mother told me. She heard it from our priest. She wasn't married to my father." Then he added, haltingly, "I never met my father."

"Where are you from, August?"

"Pristina Polje, Kosovo."

"But that is hours away from here. How did you get here?'

"I hitchhiked."

Betty recalled feelings of suspicion about Viktor hiding a secret. *Was this it? My husband has a son and never told me about it? Or could it be that this young boy had found out that I was alone at the castle this day and evening and is taking advantage of me?* But she quickly rejected this possibility. She pulled herself together and faced the situation head-on.

"Well, August, I'll tell you something. It's late, almost midnight. My husband and some guests were in Vienna today and I expect them back any minute. Why don't I fix one of our guestrooms for you and you try to sleep. We'll talk again in the morning. Right now it's time for you to go to bed." Resolutely she bade August to follow her, led him to one of the spare rooms in the east wing, put new sheets on the bed with August's help, and tucked the boy in. August smiled at her, turned around, and fell asleep even before she had left the room.

He must have been exhausted, poor boy—just lost his mother! Betty thought to herself. *Tomorrow we'll unravel this whole drama. I won't tell Viktor anything tonight. He has a lot of explaining to do, I'd say.* She called Rupert and asked him not to mention the arrival of the late visitor to Viktor.

She hurried back to the sitting room to find little Liesl still as she had left her, sleeping like an angel. Half an hour later she heard the car rolling into the garage and after a few minutes the group came up the stairs and joined her in the sitting room. Kathryn was fast asleep in Viktor's arms.

"How was your day," she asked, "and did you all enjoy the opera?"

They all wanted to talk at the same time. "Great, fantastic, wish you could have gone with us." Nobody noticed a little tenseness in Betty.

Betty put her finger to her mouth. "Pssst, please, you'll wake the baby."

Lotti took the sleeping Kathryn and put her to bed.

After they had calmed down and eaten the small *Imbiß* Frau Grete had prepared for them and had a cup of tea, Viktor took his wife and baby, apologized to the guests, and retired to their bedroom. Betty was very tired and bewildered; she did not say much except to express her joy that everybody had a good time. She quickly got ready for bed and feigned sleep when Viktor joined her. However, she could not fall asleep for a long time. All kinds of puzzling thoughts were keeping her awake. *So, Viktor had an affair before? Why didn't he tell me? Why hadn't he married August's mother? Who was that mother? What were they doing in Kosovo? What would happen tomorrow?* Finally, when she was aware of her husband's deep breathing, she also relaxed and drifted off to sleep.

CHAPTER 9

Confession

On Sunday morning the castle people usually slept longer. But Betty, who woke up when the rooster crowed at five o'clock, decided that she had to talk with Viktor right now, before everyone else was stirring. Viktor, not too pleased to be softly nudged by his wife, tried to turn to the other side, but then opened his eyes and saw the serious look on Betty's face.

"Betty, good morning, what's the matter? It's Sunday morning. Too early to wake up."

"Viktor, I have to talk to you, now." Viktor sat up.

"What could be so urgent that you deprive me of my well-earned Sunday morning sleep, my dear?"

"Viktor, it's hard to tell you, but why didn't you tell me you had a son, why didn't you?"

Viktor looked aghast. "Who told you?" he asked harshly. Then he saw her bewildered face. "I would have told you, but not right now. Now someone else told you."

"Yes, August did."

"August? But he knew that he could not come here. I had told his mother …"

"His mother just died two days ago. He had no other place to go than to his father."

Viktor's shoulders fell. "Oh! No! Adele died. I knew she was sickly. But she was still so young. Oh, why didn't I tell you?" The man, who usually was so composed and sure of himself, broke down in tears, not knowing what to say. There was nothing he could say.

Betty thought for a while. "Yes, why didn't you. I would have appreciated that. But now we have to decide what to do with August. He seems to be a nice young man." Then she decided to test him and August. "Tell me, Viktor, were you ever married to Adele? Or is August your illegitimate child? If you were married to her, I could not forgive you." She turned away from her husband.

"Adele was much younger than I. We never got married. Believe me, Betty, had I married her and I would still be her husband, I would not have married you. I am not that bad. Please, look at me. I know I made a mess of myself. Now August is affected also. I had thought that Adele could have taken care of him until he was independent. I would have always paid for his expenses. But she never contacted me. I actually forgot about her. Raphael took care of the financial arrangements." He paused for a while. "Would you be willing to let him stay with us until he is on his own?"

Betty stayed quiet for some time. Then she turned around slowly and looked her husband in the face. "I am willing to be a second mother to that nice boy. We got a little acquainted yesterday. He is sleeping in one of the guestrooms. He was exhausted. He wanted to speak to his father."

She paused for a while. Then, looking her husband straight into his eyes, she said gravely, "Viktor, you have a lot of explaining to do. But not now. We have to get up and start this day. There is time after church. Then we'll talk."

Viktor returned her gaze. "Yes, Betty, we shall talk. But first, I have to speak to my son. I only hope he will not give us any trouble. Adele was a Gypsy and he has some of that blood in him. I am so grateful to you that you will give him a chance. What will your sons say?"

"We'll see. They will be as surprised as I was, when August turned up on my doorstep." Then she added, "What my parents will say, who knows? My mother can be very understanding; but my father? He is such a straight-laced Christian. It will take time. Both of them think the world of you. But having a love child and then not telling about it?" She sighed deeply, pulled herself together and got out of bed.

The first thing she did when she was dressed was to go downstairs to the kitchen and talk to *Frau* Schwarz who was always the first up of the staff. Grete was getting the trays ready for breakfast and was astonished to see her mistress up so early.

"I thought, after yesterday's late hours, you and your husband would sleep a little longer?" she asked.

"*Frau* Schwarz, I have to talk to you." Betty began. "Did you people know about an affair my husband had with a young Gypsy girl?"

Frau Grete's face showed embarrassment. "Several people knew, but it was supposed to be a secret." She did not really know what was going on. "She was not allowed to show her face around here, neither she nor her son."

"Well, young August showed up here last night while my husband was gone. His mother had died suddenly and he wanted to see his father."

Grete's face showed pity. "You poor thing, where is that boy now? You should have wakened me; I could have put him to bed for the night."

"I gave him one of the spare rooms and he is still asleep."

Grete thought for a while. She muttered to herself. *So, that's why they were so upset the other night.* Then she said aloud, "I think this is very brave of you, *Frau* Baumeister. Not every young married woman would have handled this so well. I hope it does not ruin your marriage?" she added with a quizzical look.

Betty straightened up. "Thank you, *Frau* Schwarz. I think I can handle the situation. Would you be so kind and tell young Master August that breakfast is at eight-thirty? We'll all go to church. August can wear one of Nathan's suits. I think he is about his size. His own clothes are beyond mending."

Now her parents had to be told. Betty went upstairs again to take care of her baby who was wide awake and playing with her toes. "You little darling! You slept through all of this. Let's see what you will say to your new big brother?" She took the sopping wet little thing, bathed and dressed her, and prepared her bottle.

Meanwhile Viktor had gotten up and was bracing himself for the coming day. He also was concerned about the reaction of his parents-in-law. He was amazed at the calm and composure of his wife. They now had four children to take care of. He hoped that everything would work out. He did not realize that half the village and also his staff knew about his affair with Adele and the existence of August. But in some way he was relieved that everything was in the open now. He still had to meet his son.

August woke up when the rays of the rising sun hit his forehead. He looked around the unfamiliar room and wondered what had happened to him. Little by little his memory came back. He must be in his father's castle. The nice lady who told him that she was his father's wife—wasn't her name Betty?—had put him in this bed and told him to sleep well. The bed was so comfortable; he never had felt better. Soft mattress, clean sheets, a fluffy feather pillow (European comforter), a sweet-smelling pillow under his head, now warmed by sunrays, "Ahh, that's nice." He stretched his limbs, turned around to avoid the sun in his eyes, and started recalling what had happened to him.

Only yesterday he had still been at the camp in Pristina Polje. Why is he here now? Oh yes, Mother had died and before she turned limp in his arms, she had said, "Go to Austria, August. Find your father and have him take care of you."

August knew about his father. His mother, Adele, had told him about the Castle Blauenwald, near the small town of Leibnitz. About a week ago she had asked her son to listen carefully to what she had to say to him.

"My dear August, I should have told you much earlier, but I always thought you were too young to understand. Of course you are wondering who your father is and why he is not with us. I thought there would be plenty of time to let you know. But for several months now I've felt so weak and so sick and I know that I'll not be with you much longer. It is time for you to know what to do when I'm not here anymore." Adele had to pause and August offered her a sip of water. He took her in his arms and told her to stay calm and only talk if she felt up to it. Adele sighed and continued.

"You have to know this about your father. He and I were young and foolish when this happened. I had left the camp of my relatives and was traveling around Austria on my own. I had a job as waitress at the *Buschenschank* in Blauenwald. But I was always tired and the owner of the tavern told me I could work for one more week and then had to go. He had hired someone else who would take over for me. I didn't know what to do and decided to have one more drink at the tavern.

"It was a nice spring evening. I enjoyed just resting and sipping my drink. Then I saw your father, Viktor Baumeister, sitting at the bar with friends. They had been drinking. I was only fourteen and still, I should have known better. He saw me, got up, and came to my table where I was sitting by myself, having a drink in front of me and feeling worried about my future. He was very friendly and, oh, so good-looking. He offered to pay for my drink and invited me to walk with him in the beautiful moonlit night. I observed his friends shaking their heads. They didn't want him to talk to with me. But he ignored them and they left. He asked me to go for a walk with him. I couldn't resist. He led me to a grassy spot in the woods near Blauenwald. We sat down and he started to kiss me. When he wanted more from me than a kiss, I became afraid and wanted him to leave me alone. But he was stronger than I and so it happened. You know what I'm talking about, don't you, August. You are eleven now and almost a young man."

"Yes, Mother, I do. My father raped you and that's what happened. You became pregnant and he didn't want anything to do with you or me. I hate him. Why didn't he take care of you and me, the way he should have? Don't tell me to look for him. Don't die, please, don't leave me."

Adele sighed and pressed his hand. "I know; I don't want to leave you. But I also know that the end is near. So, do as I tell you now. You know that you and I were never really accepted by the others here because I don't have a husband. Right after the funeral you should leave the camp and find your father. He is not a bad man; he just couldn't stay with me and marry me. I forgive him and so should you. He will take you in. I know it in my heart." A coughing spell interrupted her outpour and she was unable to say anymore. A few days later she drew her last breath. August kissed her lovingly and assured her he would do what she had told him. She died with a smile on her face. He went to the village priest, who assured him that he would arrange for a funeral next week. He gathered his belongings and left the camp. He knew what to do.

Early the next morning, he hitchhiked north toward the Austrian border. A bus brought him across the border to Leibnitz where he arrived when it was getting dark. A farmer picked him up and gave him a lift to Blauenwald. He walked up the linden alley and knocked on the guard's window at the gate. Rupert called the castle and told him to go ahead, into the courtyard, up the stairs, and to knock on the second door to the left.

August remembered following Rupert's directions, knocking on the door and hearing the dog growl. He must have been very sleepy and vaguely recalled the kind looking lady who told him that she was his father's wife and that he should go to sleep. Well, and now he's had a good night's sleep behind him and faced a new future. What would his father be like? Would he acknowledge him, August, as his son? Would he, August, accept him as his father, after having been abandoned for eleven years? He had followed his dear mother's directions. He was here now, at Blauenwald, and the next hours would reveal his coming fate. He turned around once more and fell back to sleep. He woke up from a knock at the door and answered boldly, "Come in." His eyes met the friendly face of yet another new person. *Frau* Grete bade him a good morning and changed the tattered clothes on the chair by the bed with clean ones from Nathan. "Don't let me disturb you, my dear," she told him, "just go back to sleep and when you do get up, wear these," she pointed to the fresh garments, "your old ones are taken care of." Gently she left the room and closed the door quietly. August drifted back to sleep.

Viktor walked to the door of the guest room where August was still sleeping. He knocked on the door. A sleepy voice answered, "Yes."

"August, it's Viktor, your father, may I come in?"

After a long pause he heard August's voice, questioning, "Yes?"

Viktor opened the door slowly. August was sitting in his bed, rubbing his eyes.

"August, this is not easy for me. But I want you to know that you will be welcome in our home as my son. You may thank my wife Betty for that."

Nothing from August. The boy stared at his father as if he were a total stranger. Well, he *was* a total stranger to August, though the boy had thought of his father often. He *was* good-looking. His mother was right. But that didn't make any difference.

"Please say something, August. Are you willing to stay with us and consider our castle as your home from now on?"

"I'll try."

"Thank you. We all know that you lost your mother just two days ago. We feel very sorry about that."

"I loved my mother. She was my only friend."

"You'll get over it. We all want to become your friends."

Nothing from August.

"Please get dressed now and join us. Betty and I will be waiting in front of your door. Please don't make us wait too long."

Upon leaving the room, Viktor thought he detected a small nod of August's head. Viktor closed the door carefully and walked to the master bedroom where Betty waited for him. "He's dressing now. Let's go to his room." When they got to the guest room August had just opened the door and was looking around for them. His face lightened up when he saw Betty. Together they went to the dining room.

At eight-thirty the gong had sounded and the family had come together. Gerda and *Frau* Schwarz had decided to let the family eat without them and had eaten their breakfast earlier in the kitchen. Mary, Luther and Raphael were already sitting at their places, when the guests came in, one by one, first Erma and Hans with Kathryn, then Lotti and Peter. Nathan and Jacob appeared a little later, Viktor and Betty arrived last, having August between them. Everybody perceived the newcomer and wondered who he might be. Viktor addressed his family and friends.

"Good morning, folks. I want you to meet my son August. This is not easy for me. There is not much explaining I can do. August's mother died the day before yesterday in Kosovo Polje and he did the right thing. He came to his father and he will live here now with

Betty, her parents, the boys, Liesl, and me." He looked around at the quizzical faces. Then he added the thunderbolt.

"His mother and I were never married."

"Well, that's news," said Luther. He looked at his wife. "Mary, what do you think of this?"

Mary answered, "I think that Viktor should have given us at least a hint. But it looks like our Betty is okay with it and that's good enough for me." She got out of her chair, went to August and gave him a big hug. August was a little embarrassed. Nobody but his own mother had ever hugged him. Viktor's wife did not really seem to be the hugging type. And this grandmotherly lady was treating him like her own grandson. He liked it, but could not quite understand it.

Nathan and Jacob looked at each other. As far as they understood the situation, they had now sort of a brother, about their age, and a real son of their stepfather. They felt reluctant. Everybody else felt like they were watching a real live drama.

"Now when did all this happen?" asked Lotti.

"When we left yesterday morning, August wasn't here," Kathryn observed.

Erma, with her motherly instinct, followed Mary's example, and gave August a good hug. Hans acted more reserved. He offered the boy a handshake.

Betty addressed the family. "I want you all to know that nobody could have been more surprised than I when this young man showed up, just about an hour before you all came back from Vienna. Viktor and I talked it over this morning and now we have four children."

Mary could not suppress a sigh. "That's very brave of you, Betty."

"One more question," asked Luther. "What is August's last name?"

Nobody had thought of this yet. Then August spoke up, "My name is August Boraq, my mother's name." Luther thought to himself. *It should be August Baumeister. Would the boy agree to change his last name?*

CHAPTER 10

Forgiveness

Luther's question surely stirred up some serious thoughts in everyone's mind. If Viktor kept the boy as his son, he should bear the Baumeister name. But would the proud boy be willing to let this happen?

Little by little breakfast went its usual course. It had been decided to go to the morning service in the adjacent church.

At ten o'clock Viktor took his family and friends to church. Word of the news had spread throughout the household and beyond that through the village. A cluster of people was waiting in front of the church to greet the Baumeisters and the Brenners.

Nathan and Jacob, not really enthusiastic about this ritual, were going also, twelve-year-old Nathan, because he was preparing to be confirmed end of July and Jacob, because he was too young to be left at the castle by himself. Besides, Jacob wanted to be where Kathryn was and Kathryn wanted to go to church with everyone else. Baby Liesl was snug in her mother's arms. It was quite a procession walking out of the gate and down the footpath along the east wing of the castle to the entrance of the church, where the priest Raphael Garibaldi welcomed them. This cleric, who had as a young man taken confession from Viktor twelve years ago, was maybe the only person in Blauenwald who knew the details about the mystery surrounding young August. Though Manfred Sattler knew Adele well—after having been fired from her waitress job at the *Buschenschank*, she had been employed by his wife to work at Reichenfels—he had never connected the fact that Viktor asked him to dismiss her from her services to him with the rumor going around in the community of Blauenwald. But Raphael actually knew from Viktor's own confession that he had sired a child and had told Adele to leave Blauenwald forever. It was a selfish act and Viktor knew it. He did not want to tarnish his reputation. He did not even feel sorry for Adele whom he had wronged and whom he had then abandoned. He had not wanted her to give birth to the baby in Blauenwald. In fact, he would have been relieved if Adele had undergone an abortion. Since the 1960s abortions were legal. But he knew that Adele, like most people who embraced the Catholic faith, would never do such a thing.

Raphael had received a phone call from the priest in Pristina and knew that August had left Gypsytown right after his mother's death. So he hoped that all had gone well and that August would materialize somehow in Blauenwald. He was not sure how he would be received by his father.

Raphael had told Viktor again and again to inquire about Adele and his son. Most of all, he had urged Viktor to share all of this with Betty. He admired Viktor's wife very much and was sure she would forgive her husband. Up to last night Viktor had not followed this well-meant advice. He had been afraid he would lose Betty.

Therefore Raphael was very relieved to see August among the group of Baumeisters, Fromms, and Brenners. While shaking Viktor's hand, he complimented him for taking the boy, but urgently advised him to drive with August to Kosovo and attend the funeral of Adele's body. "After that you will feel closure and atonement and will be able to make good on everything you have done to this poor woman and your son. August certainly deserves not to be abandoned now and he will like to see his mother properly buried. She was the only person he was close to. If you want me to, I shall contact the priest in Kosovo Polje today to find out about plans for the funeral." His voice was urgent. "Let your wife know everything," he added.

This time Viktor did not ignore Raphael's counsel. He agreed to what his priest said and entered the church, fully aware of the added obligations he had to fulfill. *I shall tell Betty all that happened and hope she can forgive me,* he pledged to himself.

Viktor had no idea that rumors about Adele's pregnancy had been leaked by no other than his would-be enemy Sepp Wanz. That schemer had grabbed at any opportunity to tarnish Viktor's reputation and he had found willing listeners. He had heard the story from Dr. Amato whom he had trusted at that time. Half the village knew that it was young Master Baumeister's affair with the young Gypsy girl that had her disappear so suddenly and unfortunately. Dr. Amato, who had examined Adele after she came to him wondering why she did not have her monthly bleeding, had helped to substantiate the sad news.

No wonder Viktor felt that people in Blauenwald and in the castle looked away when he wanted to start a friendly conversation.

Among the congregation were Manfred Sattler and his son, Paul, who had refused to listen to the rumors about their friend. Viktor had not mentioned anything about a relationship with Adele to them; therefore they shunned the rumors and trusted Viktor's integrity. They thought that the young boy who was with the Baumeisters was one of the Brenner relatives. They were shocked when they heard the disheartening news during the service from the pulpit.

After Viktor and his son had entered the church side by side, had sat demurely down in the last row, and the people had quieted down, the priest mounted the pulpit and addressed the congregation.

"Dearly Beloved. We are gathered this morning to greet a new person in our midst. Meet August, who is finally united with his father, Viktor Baumeister …" He paused and the congregation was quiet. One could hear a pin drop and all eyes were on Raphael. He saw the expectancy in the faces of his flock and chose his next words carefully. "Let's all welcome August after the service. His mother died two days ago and he found the way to his father and he is now a part of the family at the castle. And now let's listen to God's word." Raphael had chosen the same text he had used twelve years ago, Jesus' words about forgiveness. He cited from the *Lord's Prayer:* "Forgive us our trespasses as we forgive those who trespass against us."

After the service the congregation filed past the priest who shook everyone's hand warmly and thanked them for coming. They also crowded around young August and made him feel welcome. Many of the village people were just as surprised as the castle staff had been when Raphael explained the appearance of August briefly during his sermon. *He*, the priest, of course, was intimately familiar with the story and had heard the sad news about Adele's death on Friday evening from his colleague in Kosovo Polje over the telephone. He had been at the breakfast table with the Baumeister family in the morning and knew about August's appearance the night before. He was glad to see the boy attending the service with his new family. Twelve years ago he had pressed Viktor's hand empathetically after church and he did so again today, mentioning only that he wanted to talk to him and Betty in private a little later.

People who stared curiously at the shy boy did not realize that August was still overwhelmed by all the happenings within the last days and that he felt animosity against the person who was so willing to be his father now, but had never shown any interest in them while his mother was still alive. He let Viktor hold his hand only reluctantly.

At the castle *Mittagessen* was served and after the meal Raphael had a brief meeting with Betty and Viktor in the study. He praised both of them about their decision to accept August and the three of them promised to do whatever they could to make the boy feel welcome in their family and community.

After Raphael left, Viktor and Betty had a long talk. He owed her an explanation about what had happened back in 1975 and why he had not told her about it before. They sat at Viktor's desk, under the auspices of his ancestors, the stern parents, his jovial grandfather, and his Uncle Karl, the spitting image of his father Rudolf Baumeister.

Viktor sighed deeply. "I know. I can only hope and pray that you don't turn your back on me. Please listen to me.

"I can only tell you that I was not the same person at that time. I was pretty selfish then. And after I met you, I did not want to say anything to you that might change your mind. I didn't want to lose you."

"It would have been easier for all of us if you had told me, Viktor. All I can say is that August's sudden appearance was traumatic for everyone." Then she added, "Tell me, Viktor, how *did* it happen?"

"My dear Betty, I promise to tell you the truth, but please understand that this is not easy for me. I tell you again; before I met you I was a different person. I thought more of myself and wanted nothing but an untroubled and easy life. School was just another thing that was in the way of my pleasures. I got by with as little effort as possible and thought I could continue to spend my parents' money forever. I was close to thirty years old and had invited some of my fellow students who were in the same situation as I. They would stay with me at the castle and we spent happy days together hiking, drinking, and dancing the days away. You might not believe this, Betty, but I was shy when it came to girls. I'd never had a sister and the female students in Vienna where so conceited and haughty. It was much easier to hang out with men. I had a few mistresses, but they did not satisfy me. Also they wanted lots of money. I had no real goal in life.

"It was a balmy evening in early May. The daffodils were blooming, the birds were singing, and the air was clean and fresh after a morning shower. I was feeling great and ready to conquer the world. I had come home from studying in Vienna for spring break with some friends and we wanted to have a good time. Some friends from Blauenwald joined us and talked me into visiting the *Buschenschank*; you know, that place I took you once, where everyone meets and you drink all the wine you want. It's local, cheap, and oh, so good. In the corner of the room sat a girl I had not seen before. One of my friends told me. 'Don't look at her; she is a Gypsy, just traveling through Blauenwald. It's not good to get entangled with Gypsies.'

"This perked up my curiosity. After my third glass of *Heuriger* I got up, walked over to her table, and asked if I could sit down. She lifted her head, stared at me with blazing black eyes, pulled back the heavy black hair, and invited me with a deep voice, accented with a heavy Roma accent, to sit down. We started talking and she told me that her parents had been killed by Albanian rebels when she was only eight. She was living with her relatives in Gypsytown, a suburb of Pristina.

"'Our people didn't feel safe living in the big city,' she told me. 'My folks have always been mistreated by those Muslim Albanians, who hate all Christian people. I wanted to be by myself and left them to find my future in Austria. My money ran out when I came to Blauenwald. I tried to get a job, and for a while worked here at the *Buschenschank*. But they dismissed me today. I've decided to go back to my folks in Kosovo.'

"She was so pretty that I felt I had to get closer to her. 'May I order you some wine?' I asked her, praying that she would let me treat her.

"'If you want to,' she said nonchalantly and even smiled at me. That did it. I was hopelessly in love with her. We drank more than we should have and when I looked around for my friends—they had all left. She told me that her name was Adele and that she was fourteen, almost fifteen. I was afraid to tell her who I was, just that I was Viktor, living at the castle. She asked me if I could find a job for her at the castle and I told her I might. She did not know that I was the son of the owners nor did she know my age. I was almost twice her age! I hardly remember how it happened. We went for a walk in the moonlight and found a nice grassy place to sit down. Adele was so pretty—I couldn't help myself. She struggled a bit but I was stronger than she. When it was over, she cried. I brought her to a little hotel, paid for a night's stay for her, and left.

"I found her a job at our friend Manfred's farm and went back to Vienna.

"After two months I came home again to visit my parents and drove over to Reichenfels to inquire about Adele. She was still there and we met again. It was then that she told me she was expecting a child and that I was definitely the father. I was very shocked; it hit me like a bolt of lightning. I did not want to marry the girl. I was from a good Austrian family, and would some day be the owner of the castle. She was a Gypsy. I should not have become entangled with her. I had been drunk and now I had to deal with the consequences. I scraped all my money together, gave it to her and told her to leave the area and go back to her people. I really did not treat her well. I told Manfred to dismiss her, which he did reluctantly, and bought a train ticket to Pristina for her. There was nothing Adele could do but obey me. The money I gave her would be enough to take care of her and the baby at least for a while. I never heard from her again. I confessed my sin to Raphael (he left out the fact that this happened two months after the insult had happened, after Adele had gone to Dr. Amato, and after he had learned that she was pregnant) and took penance. I allowed a fixed sum to be sent to her and had Raphael handle the entire thing. I tried to forget about her and her son and went on with my life."

He took a deep breath and said beseechingly, "Then I met you and I did not want to bring up this dark chapter of my past. I was afraid I would lose you. Can you understand that, Betty, and forgive me?"

Betty, who had listened attentively facing the wall, was quiet for a while. Then she turned toward Viktor and said, "I understand and I am not turning my back on August. I am trying hard to forgive you, Viktor. Please understand that the last few hours have not been easy for me. I am only afraid that August might not be so forgiving. He has to find a way to figure out why you sent his mother away and did not want to have anything to do with your son except sending money for her upkeep."

Then she asked, "How could you go on with your life without telling anybody, especially me?"

"I confessed my sin to Raphael as soon as I knew about it and did penance." He could feel the shallowness of this response. "After that I had a serious talk with him, but did not take his advice, and continued with my former life."

"Oh, Viktor, how could you?"

"I don't know, Betty. I let the priest handle it. It was not before I lost both parents that I suffered the first pangs of a guilty conscience. I had never told them. They died without knowing what I had done. And then you came into my life. I did not want to lose you. Raphael told me again and again to approach Adele and meet my son, but I was not strong enough to do it. He also told me to talk to you about it. And now Adele's death has left me no choice.

"That's all that I can tell you, Betty. Can you really forgive me?"

Imploringly he touched her hand, not daring to spoil the sacred moment. Betty turned toward the wall again and was quiet for a long time. Did she love Viktor enough to forgive him? What could she do? So many people's lives would be affected by her decision. Her own sons had just gotten used to having a father again. Her parents? What would happen to them? And little Liesl? Betty could not think any further. She had to stay with Viktor. She had to try to forgive him. It would not be easy. She turned around and looked at him fully.

"Viktor, Adele's death leaves me no choice either. It happened and I will do my best. The truth is out now; that's good. I hope there are no more secrets?"

"No more secrets, Betty. This one is more than enough."

Meanwhile the sun had gone down and it was time for the evening meal. So Betty would forgive Viktor; but would August ever forget that his father had abandoned him?

CHAPTER 11

August

During the afternoon it rained on and off. Everyone had their own agenda: Luther and Mary strolled through the vineyard during breaks in the weather; the Brenners and Kathryn met in the sitting room and spent the afternoon relaxing, reading, and playing games. The boys took off together to investigate the stables. August liked the castle and the grounds very much. So much room and everything so comfortable!

"Let's have something to eat," suggested Jacob. The three boys went to the kitchen and soon found Hanni who prepared a nice *Jause* for them.

After they had eaten, the boys found a cozy corner in the staff dining room and started to talk.

Jacob asked, "So, August, you will now be living with us, sort of like our brother? We are sorry that your mother died. That must be hard." August nodded.

Nathan added, "But you have your father now. We've lost our father. I was five and Jacob was too little to remember him. I always wished he would still be alive."

August thought about that. "I am sorry you've lost your father. But you have your real mother. I lost mine. She was so good and so sweet. Why did she have to die?"

"But now you are with your *real* father," said Jacob. "I like Viktor very much. I wish he was my real father. Now you have us, sort of as brothers."

August nodded his head. "Oh yes, you are my stepbrothers. That's all very nice. But I will always miss my mother. We were so very close."

Nathan intervened, "You'll learn to like our mother too. She is a good person. She might even be better than your mother."

Jacob felt that Nathan was too abrupt. "Nathan, don't say that. You didn't even know August's mother. August, tell us about her."

August mused, "She was always so pretty and smelled so good."

Nathan, on the defense, "Our mother is pretty, too."

"I know, but in a different way. My mother was so … warm and loving and … I'm sorry, I don't want to talk about my mother anymore."

Jacob looked around. "I think it's not raining right now. Nathan, let's go out to the woods and look for the hedgehog. Have you ever seen a real hedgehog, August?"

"Of course, we had one living under our tent and my mother fed him. One year we had a large family. But they all disappeared."

The boys took off for the woods.

August had left the two others roaming around for the hedgehog and slowly walked back to the castle. It surely was a wonderful place. But would he get used to the people here? Would it last? His mother had wanted him to go to his father at the castle. Well, he did. Now he had to see what would happen next. He thought about the two boys, his stepbrothers. At least those two spoke his language. Though he could hardly understand them. Those other two young people from California, Peter and Lotti, were just learning to speak German. And that little girl? She only babbled in German. But all that didn't really matter. How could he ever get over the fact that his father had abandoned him all this time? Only when his mother died and he had no place else to go, had his father acknowledged him. Why not before that? His mother would have been so happy. Did his mother die of grief? That he could never forgive. He was only here because his mother wanted him to be.

He had reached the gate and heard Rupert greet him. "Good afternoon, Master August, how do you like our castle?"

"I like the castle fine," was August's diplomatic answer. Trudging up the big staircase, he met *Frau* Grete who also greeted him friendly.

"Getting to know this place, Master August?"

"Yes, it sure is big, *Frau* Grete," he answered with a lame smile and went on. Grete shook her head and thought it queer that he wasn't playing with the other boys. *Is he a loner?* She asked herself. *Poor guy, he just lost his mother. It must be hard.* She decided to always be nice to him and to make him feel welcome. She knew that Gerda and all of their staff agreed with her. *It isn't his fault.*

One thing was for sure. The *Spuk,* that had been so loud all through Friday night, had finally stopped making a racket. So everything would turn out all right.

When *Frau* Schwarz came back to her kitchen, Peter Brenner was chatting with some of the helpers who were busy getting ready for the evening meal. She greeted him. "Hello, Master Peter, what can we do for you?"

"*Frau* Schwarz, could I ask you some questions?" Peter had improved his knowledge of Austrian German a great deal and was able to understand now most of what the "natives" were saying.

"Sure. Just let me talk to the girls and then the two of us have a nice chat. Please, sit down." She motioned him to the chair next to her desk and joined him after telling her helpers what to do for tonight's *Abendbrot.*

"So, what's on your mind, Master Peter?"

"*Frau* Schwarz, I am just curious. Did you know about August? Did anyone around here know about him? You have been at the castle for so long. Would you mind telling me?" And when *Frau* Grete seemed a little hesitant, he used his sure-fire method when interviewing people—he flattered her. "You can't really blame me for being interested in our good friends' lives. And you seem to me a reliable person whom I can trust. I don't want to bother the Baumeisters now. You'll understand that!"

Frau Grete *did* feel flattered and she relaxed. "Well, Master Peter, it's a long story. I have a little time now, so here is what I know." She poured a cup of tea for Peter.

"I think you know about our master's grandparents."

Peter nodded. "I heard about this when I was a teenager and Viktor told us about his castle."

"So, their names were Rudolf and Maria…," here *Frau* Grete halted, but then continued. "They had two sons, Alfred and Karl. Well, they bought this castle and hired me as a housekeeper in 1922. The *Spuk* was pretty busy then and the castle didn't look like it does now. It looked rather bad and neglected. But within ten years or so it was in much better shape, so good that the Nazis wanted Blauenwald to become their headquarters at the *Anschluß*.

"I know all about the *Anschluß* in 1938," Peter interrupted. "Hitler wanted to annex Austria and make it a province of Germany. Chancellor Kurt von Schuschnigg was a weak man and just handed Austria over to the Nazis. We learned about all that in history class."

"But *Frau* Maria chased them away. Oh yes, she was quite a strong lady! In 1939 World War II broke out and their son Karl was drafted. Alfred was older and wasn't drafted. He was studying in Vienna, where he had married Susanne Fischer, a girl from southern Germany."

Peter exclaimed, "That's my 'Aunt' Susanne, my mother's first cousin. Yes, she is Viktor's mother. My mother told me about her. You know, Viktor visited us in California many times."

Frau Grete nodded. "I know, but didn't you want to know about Master August?"

"Yes, I do," said Peter.

Frau Grete took a deep breath and bent a little closer to Peter. "There had been these rumors that Master Viktor and this Gypsy girl, Adele, had something going on." She looked at the girls who were busy preparing for supper.

"Let's talk very quietly. *Little pitchers have big ears.*" She whispered. "Can you understand me?"

Peter nodded.

"Some people in the village were talking about it, but most of them had no idea. So, when Master August appeared out of nowhere, some people in Blauenwald put two and two together. Well, do you understand that all of this is not easy for us at the castle? I hope that young *Frau* Betty can live with it. It happened so suddenly. I really do like her and hope she can forgive her husband. They have her two sons, their own little one, and now this boy."

"Oh, Betty is great," Peter reassured her. "I've always admired her."

Just then Gerda came into the kitchen, saw *Frau* Grete and Peter talking together, and approached them. "Sorry to interrupt. It's time for *Abendbrot*. Shall I let the people know?"

Frau Grete looked at the clock. "Well, I'll be darned. Sorry, Master Peter, we have to stop our little chat. Could you excuse me?"

Peter had heard all he wanted. He thanked *Frau* Grete politely for her time and went upstairs to get ready for the evening meal.

August became a regular member of the castle household. He was a beautiful boy, strong, straight, (his little stoop was gone with healthy exercise at school and play) with dark curly hair and black eyes, like his mother. But he brooded a lot. Never did he forget how the people in Kosovo had treated them like an outcast. As long as his mother was alive he had participated in the activities at the camp, had loved dancing and singing, also performing in plays for the villagers. Everyone had contributed to the welfare of the community, with crafting jewelry, repairing household goods, and foretelling the future. The colorful costumes they wore, the way they treated the sick, and their peculiar ways of worshipping had impressed the boy deeply. In many ways he longed to be back with his kind, but he had never felt quite accepted by them. He now felt blessed to have a father and siblings. However, he would never be completely one of them. Just like in Kosovo, his hot temper got him into trouble at times, but usually he was reserved and uncommitted. He tried not to interfere with other people's business. The town people could never forget, though, that he was a Gypsy, born out of wedlock. A nobody, really. As usual, the woman was mainly to blame. His beautiful mother, his only real friend, who was a victim of rape.

On the Monday after August's arrival at the castle, Viktor arranged for himself and August to go to Kosovo Polje and, together with the village priest, organized a proper funeral that was scheduled for the following day. Only a handful of people, mostly Romas, attended. Adele was laid to rest in the cemetery adjoining the little church in the village.

Though pleased that his mother was now officially buried, August did not find closure in his heart concerning his father. He decided to never call him "Father" nor "Viktor" and would avoid addressing him personally in the future. Viktor felt that he had done everything possible and hoped to win August's love eventually. In spite of the fact that August was his own flesh and blood, he was much more comfortable with his stepsons, especially Jacob.

August was enrolled in school and grew accustomed to his new life. After a few months he began to feel better about himself and made friends. The people in the community became accustomed to him and he was accepted as a part of the Baumeister family, though he clung to the "Boraq" name. But that his last name was not "Baumeister" didn't matter much. After all, Betty's two sons were not Baumeisters either. They were Goldsteins. Still, it all was one big family. The only real Baumeister was little Liesl. She adored her new-found half-brother and followed him around wherever he went. The only person whom August could never get really comfortable with was Viktor, his father. There was something between them—a deep rift that could not be repaired. August could not forgive his father and Viktor was unable to mend that rift. He wished he could.

The Brenners left Austria after having stayed at the castle for three weeks and spent three more weeks in Germany. Lotti decided that she did not want to stay away from her husband any longer and took little Kathryn, who had become homesick, with her. Aunt and niece became very close during this trip together.

The years went by and other problems developed around the castle.

BOOK 3

1991

CHAPTER 12

Raphael

In order to receive a milder sentence, one of the men guilty of the wine-scandal in the 1980s had leaked Sepp's name to the judge. Since Sepp was too shrewd to have had participated in the making of the poison, and had only contributed to taint the bland-tasting wine of the early 1980s harvests with sweet chemicals, the prosecution did not propose a life sentence for him, but had him serve four years in prison and put him on probation thereafter. Sepp's skillful lawyer also convinced the judge that Sepp was needed at the castle.

Josef Wanz had to go to prison in 1987 and was sent to Graz to be incarcerated at the penitentiary in that city, the capital of Styria. During that time he was allowed to have visitors. Besides his sister and occasional visits by Viktor and Paul, who still relied on Sepp's expertise about managing the Blauenwald estate, it was Raphael who made it his task to see Sepp on a regular basis. Was it his good influence—the personnel at the prison welcomed the priest's frequent visits—or had Sepp come to his senses on his own? He became a model prisoner. He was dismissed after serving his sentence with a record of good behavior in March of 1991. He had had enough time to think about his goals in life and came back to Blauenwald a changed man.

The first thing he did upon coming home was to go to his former house at the foot of the castle. It was locked. Nobody came to the door when he knocked. He knew that Paul was occupying it now. It was ten o'clock in the morning and Paul would be outside, working. A strange feeling overcame him, standing here, knocking on the door which had been his for many years and not being able to enter. He decided to try later in the day and to see Berta first. She had visited him a few times, together with Gerda who came regularly once a week. Berta had found another job, but at least would be willing to talk to him. He was lucky. She was home, tending to her mother who was ill.

"Now look who the cat dragged in." she greeted him nonchalantly. "Who would of thought to meet you again, after all this time in the slammer?"

"Yes, I'm back and thanks for the nice welcome, Berta." He was bitter about the way she treated him—his former mistress! She had not bothered to visit him more than a few times in prison.

"So, what can I do for you? I guess Gerda told you that I'm now working for Dr. Amato. Real classy man, eddicated too. He and Frieda have a real nice house. Never thought I would ever get such a nice position. If you think …"

"If you mean that I would want you back, you better think twice," Sepp interrupted. He thought that he detected a little huff in her bragging about the job with a medical doctor. "I wouldn't even take you back if you asked me to on your knees. But what I really would like from you is to tell me how things are going now up at the castle since young Master August has come back."

Berta changed her tune. She loved gossip and now came her opportunity to tell all about the latest news. "Come in, Sepp. There's a lot to tell." After she had told her mother, who had asked in a querulous tone who had come to visit, that Sepp and she wanted to talk in the kitchen, she made a pot of tea and both sat down at the kitchen table.

"Y'know, Sepp, all that stuff with young Master August happened the same year you went to the slammer. Gerda must of told you something about it. Things are going well up there, but Master Viktor and his son ain't getting on so good. He don't like his father and there's nothing Master Viktor can do about. *Frau* Grete tells me that she feels sorry about the whole mess. The *Gnädige Frau* is working her tail off with those four children. She is still pretty haughty with us Blauenwald people. But Grete says it's getting better. Isn't her fault about that thing with young Master August. My new boss, DOCTOR Amato, likes the people up at the castle. He goes there quite often now that *Herr* Luther is so sick."

Sepp was shocked. "Old *Herr* Fromm? Yes, he would be in his eighties now."

"Oh yeah, at least. He can't walk anymore. It's a pity. Folks see the old missus pushing his wheelchair and little Liesl and that old dog going along through the fields. We all like that old man. But he won't be with us much longer."

Sepp had heard enough. "Well, Berta, thanks for telling me all this. I hope your mother feels better soon. Have to go now. Thanks for the tea." And he left, knowing that his affair with Berta was over forever. He walked toward the castle and slowly climbed up the linden alley.

When he got to his old home, he saw the front door wide open. He looked inside. Paul was sitting at the kitchen table, a cup of coffee in front of him, reading the newspaper.

Sepp took a deep breath, "Good afternoon, Paul, may I come in?"

Paul looked up, startled. "Hey, Sepp, did they let you out? Sure, come in. Some coffee? I just made it."

Sepp entered and sat down. "I was released this morning. Trying to get the feel again. Thought I'd visit the old home. Gerda told me that you're living here now."

"Yes. So, what are your plans now that you have this all behind you?"

"Don't know yet. I would like to work here again."

"We sure could use your expertise, Sepp." Paul thought for a while. After filling Sepp's cup he said, "You know, Viktor is much more involved in all the work around Blauenwald than before you got into all that trouble." Paul looked a little embarrassed. He was sitting across from the former manager who did so well with the estate but so poorly when it came to managing his own affairs.

Sepp, sensing Paul's insecurity, wanted to ease the tension. "Paul, I had enough time to think things over. It was my own fault and now I feel that I see things differently. I would love to work for Viktor again. And I don't want to take your job away. I could go to Viktor and ask him to take me back. I would be satisfied to work alongside you—or even under you," he added, with down-cast eyes, almost inaudibly.

Paul, looking a little doubtful, advised Sepp to talk to Viktor.

Sepp hesitated. "I might. But first I have to get my bearings. Would you let me stay here for a little while?'

"Of course, Sepp. I could always go back to Reichenfels."

"I know. But I would prefer if you'd stay and we get acquainted a little better. After all, if I ask Viktor to take me back, I have to know if we two can get along. Do you understand what I'm saying, Paul?"

"I do. Let's give it a try."

So, after his talk with Viktor—referred to in the next chapter— Sepp moved in with Paul and to the amazement of the people in Blauenwald, the two became good friends. However, Paul did not stay together with Sepp for very long. Something else was happening and this time a letter from the Vatican in Rome stirred up a whole new chain of events.

Raphael received his call from Rome just a few days after Sepp was dismissed from prison. The priest was delirious with happiness. He was on the way to achieving his goal! For the first time since he knew of Gerda's feelings for him he intended to have a long talk with her.

Gerda had heard the news in church, when Raphael informed the congregation about his promotion and his leaving Blauenwald within the next few days. "A replacement for me is arriving soon. His name is Nathaniel. He is the best man the Holy Church could find to fill my place here in Blauenwald."

Everyone was stunned. Gerda felt as if her life was ending. She *had* to talk to Raphael. She had just returned to her room, sat down on her bed, and contemplated how to arrange a talk with her beloved when she heard a soft knock on her door.

"Come in," she whispered and Raphael entered the room.

"Gerda, I have to talk to you." He pulled up a chair and sat down opposite her. He took her hands in his. She said, barely audibly, "I know."

"You heard what I said in church. It's happening now. What I always wanted and prayed for is happening. I'll be working in Rome and will follow my destiny. Gerda, you must listen to me now." Gerda lifted her head and looked at him fully.

She said haltingly, "You know that I had you in my heart all these years. I don't think that I will ever forget you. But the church will be your fulfillment and so be it. I will learn to be happy for you. And I will follow your advice. He has been waiting for me patiently all these years."

Without even mentioning Paul's name, Gerda had understood what Raphael's advice would be. He nodded gravely. "Yes, Gerda, you have been reading my thoughts. If I would not belong to God, I certainly would have been allowed to appreciate your great love for me. I, too, will never forget you either. I wish you and Paul a happy life together. You deserve the best, Gerda. I will not stay to officiate at your wedding. It would be too difficult for me. Nathanial knows about everything, Gerda. I confessed to him that I am not as unfeeling as I should be. I am only human."

Gerda buried her face in her hands. "Goodbye, Raphael, and always include me in your prayers."

The priest kissed her hands gently, got up and left the room.

The next Sunday mass was led by the new, younger cleric who was welcomed by the congregation. Raphael was on his way to Rome.

Gerda did not wait long. She was still in her Sunday morning finery and walked out of the castle gate, down the linden alley and knocked on Paul's door. He and his father were sitting at the kitchen table, having a little *Jause*. Sepp was working outside. This was the same place Gerda had sat across from her brother exactly ten years ago. He had wanted her to marry Viktor, absurd! And then he had mentioned Paul's love for her. Well, she would follow his brotherly advice now. Or would it be too late?

When he heard the knock on the door, Paul got up and opened, surprised to see Gerda. "Come in, welcome in my little home."

Manfred, whose intuition told him that it would be better to leave these two alone now, grabbed his hat, said a few words of thanks for the food, and left.

Paul started. "What might bring you here, Gerda?"

"I just had a talk with Raphael …"

"He's leaving. I feel sorry for you."

"Yes, he's leaving. And you should not feel sorry for me." She took a deep breath. " Paul, do you still love me?"

"More than ever." He looked at Gerda's smiling face. "Could it really be true? Are you willing to marry me now?"

"If it's not too late, Paul. I wouldn't blame you if it were. But I hope you will still take me as your wife."

Paul could not suppress his utter glee. He kissed Gerda's hands, then her mouth, then took her in his arms and squeezed her so hard that she had to disentangle herself gently. She then stretched out her arms and embraced Paul, returning his kiss.

After a little while Paul said, "I know, Gerda, what this means for you. I do understand that you might never quite get over your love for Raphael. But you are making me so happy. So very happy. Come, let's go to Reichenfels and tell Father."

Of course Manfred was happy for his son. But he had his doubts. He knew that Paul's love for Gerda, though she was a few years older, was genuine. But he also knew that it was more of a decision of convenience on Gerda's side. He liked the young woman and hoped that it would be a good marriage and that she would learn to respect the younger man for his good character. He also knew that her first love for the priest would never go away. He was a wise old man.

And so Gerda and Paul got engaged, put up their banns on the church bulletin board, and set a wedding date. Raphael sent his congratulations from Rome and Nathanial officiated at the ceremony. The Baumeister family, the entire castle staff, and the community of Blauenwald had a big celebration that lasted for three days. Gerda and her brother switched rooms and everyone was happy. Sepp now lived at the castle, but as the other servants, took his meals downstairs. He did not feel that he belonged upstairs.

Everyone was happy—with one exception. Young August, now fifteen years old, had not gotten any closer to his father since he had come to the castle in 1987. In fact; the rift had deepened.

CHAPTER 13

California

It had been four years now that August had lost his mother and had found his way to the castle. His two stepbrothers had been in contact with some of their friends in California and every now and then a pink letter arrived at the castle addressed to Jacob Goldstein, which the recipient hoarded with great care. August, who was curious about what the sender could have to say to Jacob, had asked him point-blank, who this person was. Jacob could not hide a little blush. Nathan, who overheard the conversation, pulled August aside.

"It's his girlfriend. Those two have had it for each other ever since I can remember. If you know what I mean. But she's a wild one. She has lots of spunk. I like her too. She has a great voice. But she has only eyes for Jacob."

Then he thought a little. "You have met her. Do you remember the little girl who was with the Brenners when you came to the castle?"

"Let's see," August tried to remember. "Oh yeah, little Kathryn. They all left soon after I came. I didn't really get to know her. Everything was so new to me then. So she still writes to Jacob. Guess those letters are in English. Still remember how to read and write in English?"

"What d'you think? Of course. Both of us and Mother too, still know English. Next year we'll have it in school, too." So August was aware of some girl half around the world who had kept up writing to his brothers and was still interesting them. Though he was now fifteen years old, his experience with girls was still a little scanty. Of course, he loved Liesl, his little sister, but she was only five. It was the older girls that scared him. They seemed to be so cocksure of themselves. August almost envied Jacob his girlfriend.

When Viktor told his family in spring of 1991 that he wanted to visit his friends in California for a few weeks this summer and that he would take the three boys with him, he stirred up a flurry of excitement.

"Are we going to meet the Carltons?" Jacob and Nathan asked almost simultaneously.

"Yes, we are. We'll be staying with the Brenners and visit the Carltons often. It's not far; only two BART stations and then just a few steps. We'll even have a nice weekend at their lakeside cabin in the mountains, with all the family."

"Does Kathryn know?" asked Jacob, his face beaming.

"I don't know. It's still in the planning stage. Kathryn might not even be interested in you guys. She'll have her own friends."

"Betty, did you know this?" August asked his stepmother. He still called Betty by her name. "Mother" was his own and unforgettable mother in Kosovo.

"Of course. Your father and I have discussed this plan. We decided that just you men are to go. Grandma Marie, Liesl, and I are staying here and taking care of the castle."

August's face dropped. "Liesl's not going! I'll miss her."

"I know," said Betty. "But she is a little too young. And someone has to stay and look after things.

Little Liesl hugged closely to her mother. "I want to stay with Mom," she whispered.

Viktor looked at the boys. "We'll go as soon as school is out. Most likely middle of July. Jacob and Nathan, why don't you teach your brother some English and tell him about what to expect in America."

Now Mary spoke up. "I think it will be great for August to know a little English when he starts taking it next term in school. Everyone here has to learn English. He won't be so frustrated with the new language. You don't find many people in America speaking fluent German. So you better be prepared."

Betty said to the boys, "Remember when you came here in '85 and couldn't speak a word of German? Wasn't that hard?"

"But that's been six years ago, Mom,"

"And now you almost forgot your English," Viktor said.

"Not so," protested Jacob. "I've been writing to Kathryn a lot and all in English.

"I think that Kathryn will appreciate your effort to speak her language," Viktor intervened. He had said the right thing.

When he looked into the library a little later, the three boys sat together closely, having an English grammar book between them, and Jacob and Nathan teaching August the rudiments of English pronunciation. Betty had given them a few easy-to-read children's books and they were studying diligently.

The news traveled quickly. The boys told their classmates in school: "Guess what we are planning for our vacation this year: the four MEN in our family are taking off to California." Soon all the staff as well as the villagers knew about where the castle people were going in the summer. Manfred and Paul thought it was a great idea. Many people in Blauenwald knew about the relatives in California and the planned reunion in 1995. Fay Foster and the Duboises of the Lake Dwellers in California had put their heads together and had decided that it would be nice to celebrate this event in Austria. After, of course, Viktor had offered the castle for the big party. The older people in Blauenwald remembered the Brenners' visit in 1987 and little Kathryn Carlton. *Frau* Grete was anxious to see Peter and Lotti again and looked forward to comfortable chats at her kitchen desk. But they had to wait four years for the reunion to happen.

Before he could leave his estate for a few weeks, Viktor had to have his management in order. A few days after Sepp's release from prison he sat in his office and looked at his finances. It had been a good year so far: the grapes looked good, and the money for the trip to California was available. It would be the first time that he left Blauenwald after he had married and brought his family to his castle. Was Paul Sattler really capable of running the large premises single-handed?

While he was still musing, he heard a knock on his door. He asked, "Who's there?" The door opened haltingly and Sepp, cap in hand, stood in the frame.

It would not be easy for Sepp to start all over. All his savings were confiscated and he had to decide what to do with his life. After much contemplation and also asking the new priest and Paul for advice, he made up his mind to talk to Viktor. He knew that he could only be happy right here, at the castle. He had never worked any place else. It would not be easy to convince Viktor that he had changed and had given up all his former ambitions. Sepp realized that it had not been Viktor's fault that his crime was discovered. He remembered sitting one evening during the early '80s in the *Buschenschank* and having a beer with Dr. Amato. Not used to alcohol—though having to suffer four years of prison because of participating in an alcohol tainting operation—he had a little too much to drink. He must have talked about his plans then. It was his foolish trust in Dr. Amato's integrity. He would avoid that man in the future. But Viktor's lawyer, now his too, had told him that it was one of the other guys who had turned him in. *Whatever, what's done is done.* He would talk to Viktor about taking him back and letting him work again on his estate, the only place he could really call home.

Viktor was surprised when Sepp showed up at his office and politely asked for an interview. "Good morning, Viktor. As you must've heard, they released me from prison to come home to Blauenwald. I'm sorry to have let you down. Would you consider having me work again for you?"

Viktor was reluctant. "Well, Sepp, glad to have you back. You know that Paul Sattler is now my manager and he is doing a fine job."

Sepp swallowed his pride. "I know, Gerda informed me. I would be willing to work alongside Paul. Or even under him," he added haltingly. "Maybe he could use my expertise to run the place. You have been lucky not to have any major things happening. I know the estate inside out. You would not have to pay me much. I understand that Gerda finally decided to give in to Paul and marry him. Because the priest got that call to Rome." He took a deep breath and looked at Viktor pleadingly.

Viktor scratched his head. "Well, Sepp, you really got me there. I had always trusted you with my estate, but you surely misused that trust. Mmm … But after these four years in prison," and he looked Sepp straight into the eyes "you seem to have become a new man. How can you convince me to trust you again?"

"That's just it, Viktor; you have to take my word for it. Why don't you try me for a few weeks? I talked to Paul and he's all for it. He's letting me live with him in my old house until the two get married. I'm staying there right now. After the wedding I'd either find a room at the village or move to Gerda's room up here, if that's okay with you."

Viktor sat up straight. Sepp had asked him at the right time. They really could use his help this summer when he was gone. "Tell you what, Sepp, I'll think it over. I have to talk to Paul and if he is okay with you working under him, it's okay with me. Please understand, you would be working as Paul's assistant. Is that clear?"

Sepp's broad face changed into a smile. "I had to think a lot in that place, Viktor. I do understand. It'll work. I promise. Hope to gain your trust again. And, also, I'll go to church from now on. I already talked to Nathaniel."

"You mean the new priest whom the council hired for Raphael for our congregation? That's good. Hope he stays on forever. He's a good man. Almost as good as Raphael."

Viktor made a motion to continue his desk work and Sepp was dismissed. He didn't know yet that Viktor was leaving Blauenwald for three weeks during summer. Actually Viktor was relieved to have Sepp working with Paul while he was in California.

A few days later Sepp was re-employed and after the wedding he and Gerda switched rooms.

Meanwhile life went on in the castle.

While August got along well enough with his two stepbrothers, he was absolutely infatuated by his little half-sister, Liesl. It was obvious that she had inherited many good traits from her mother and also the sunny disposition from her father. She was now five years old and was already becoming the much needed glue holding the heterogeneous parts of the Baumeister family together. When August was brooding, she came along, putting her cool little hands on his forehead and coaxed a smile out of him. While the Goldstein brothers could be rough with her, her Boraq brother treated her gently, like an expensive musical instrument. Like her mother, Liesl had an even temper and hardly ever showed anger or other negative emotions. She was a well-contented child and radiated cheerfulness to others. Somehow she had inherited the happiness genes of the Fischer family. Lotti, the daughter of Erma Brenner, born Fischer, and Viktor, the son of Erma's cousin Susanne Fischer, later Alfred Baumeister's wife, were genuine happy people. They must have inherited their sunny disposition from some common ancestor. Liesl skipped around castle and grounds and like a sunbeam brought smiles to sorrowful faces. The grandparents Mary and Luther adored her. She could sit patiently for hours with Luther, now in a wheelchair because of his arthritis. After *Frau* Grete's husband, Fritz, had passed away, Luther had inherited the wheelchair and was glad to take advantage of the ramp built by Viktor's parents. Mary was still sturdy on her feet and often the two old people, Mary pushing Luther, Liesl holding on to Mary's arm, and the aging German shepherd Peter accompanying them, were seen ambling through vineyards and fields. For these old people the little girl brought back their younger years in California when Betty was Liesl's age.

Betty had not hired a new housekeeper and was busy handling all the work by herself. She was grateful that Gerda—who now had a husband to care for—offered to come up to the castle for several hours a week to help with the chores. The young village girls appreciated Betty's quiet authority and performed as well as under Gerda's stricter tutelage.

One cloudy morning in late May of 1991, not long after Sepp's return from prison and the big wedding of Paul and Gerda, when the grapes where starting to form into bunches, and the fields were heavy with ripening harvest, Luther did not feel very well. When Mary asked him if he would like to go for a stroll with her, he said, "I don't feel so good, Mary. Could you please call Dr. Amato?"

When the doctor came in, Luther was already half delirious and he could hardly recognize the familiar faces around him.

Liesl was beside herself. "Why is Grandpa so strange?" she asked her Grandmother. Betty joined the group. "Let's hope he makes it through the night," she said. She knew the signs of approaching death. She had been with David when he passed away in her arms after the SWAT car had brought the severely injured man in. She was prepared for the worst. Mary was praying silently. For her it was worse than for the others. She would now be alone. Luther died an hour before midnight. He did not have to suffer much.

"Thank God for that," murmured *Frau* Grete who had come in silently after she had noticed that something was not right when no one of the family came to the dining room, though the gong had sounded. She also knew that something bad would happen today since the *Spuk* had made a racket.

When it was over, Mary closed Luther's eyes and Viktor, who had been in the back of the room all the time, ordered everyone to leave the room so Betty could be alone with her parents. Mary and Betty sat up all night with the dead man, now so peaceful and almost looking happy. On the next Sunday Luther was buried in the family vault, next to Viktor's parents.

Mary, who was a few years younger than her late husband, was still able to care for herself and continued to be a consoling element at the castle. Gerda made it her task—at least for a few weeks after Luther's death—to look in on Mary daily to see how the old lady was doing and helping her when needed. Paul did not mind playing second fiddle for a while.

Soon after Luther was laid to rest, it was time for the planned trip to California. They left right after school was closing for summer vacation and arrived at the San Francisco Airport on a rainy day—strange weather for the usual arid summers of California. Peter, still living with his parents, drove Hans and Erma Brenner to the airport to pick up the visitors from Austria. At the Brenners' Oakland house all the Carltons were gathered to welcome them. Erma had prepared a good meal and Richard and Heidi with their three children had the dining room table set for a wonderful dinner. The usual quiet house was brimming with happy people.

"Sorry we have to eat inside, but we are really happy about this rain," Hans apologized. "Now we don't have to water outside."

"We'll have a barbecue as soon as the weather gets better," Erma promised.

Viktor assured them that they also had dry summers and appreciated occasional rains. "We have Mediterranean climate just like you do."

After a dessert of apple pie and ice cream the Carltons left and the Austrians were shown to their respective sleeping arrangements. "I thought that Viktor and August could have Lotti's old room and Jacob and Nathan might like the den." The "den" had been Heidi's room and was now used as a family room, with a pool table, computers, and a TV. It had a comfortable leather sofa that converted to a bed. Viktor looked a little dubious. How would he and August get along?

August solved the problem easily. He simply ignored his father. For the entire three weeks of their stay in California father and son did not converse except if absolutely necessary. Fortunately no one noticed. Almost every day the young people went over to the Carltons who lived just two short BART stations away or the families planned outings together. Viktor found it impossible to break through the barrier that existed between himself and his son. He felt much closer to his stepsons, especially Jacob.

Kathryn had been very excited about the visitors. She had brushed up on her German, but felt relieved when the boys spoke English with her. Heidi hoped that Kathryn would behave nicely and she was amazed how well the now ten-year-old girl was able to handle the teenage boys. However, she was worried that her daughter was too friendly with all three of them, mostly August, whom she didn't trust.

The three weeks went by quickly. While the boys had not cared much about Kathryn when she visited the Baumeisters in 1987, they were now very impressed with the vivacious girl. All four males were in love with her. Viktor could not get enough talking with her or romping around, much like his three sons. Nathan, August, and Jacob, now sixteen, fifteen, and thirteen, tried their best to woo her. Like Paris confronted with the choice of three goddesses, Kathryn was challenged to judge her pursuers. It was Nathan's idea. He had studied Greek mythology in his literary class in high school and had told the two other boys about the judgment story. They actually asked her to perform like the young man in the Greek story and have an apple in her hand.

Nathan told her, "You give that apple to your favorite guy. Now who will be the lucky one?" After looking seriously from one to the other, and a little indecision, she gave the apple to Jacob. He beamed.

"But I love all three of you. Only that Jacob and I have been friends for so long."

She was challenged and she was up to the challenge. She knew just how to keep all three of the young men captivated. And her "Uncle" Viktor simply adored her. The teenagers followed Kathryn wherever she went.

Heidi watched the young people and was amused how skillfully her daughter was able to keep all three boys interested in her. As soon as the weather turned better, the Brenners invited the family to the promised barbecue at their Oakland home. They had a nice garden with a spacious lawn and an open fire pit in the center. After the picnic, when everyone had settled comfortably around the campfire, roasting marshmallows and relaxing, they talked about what had happened during the last four years and what would happen in another four years.

Viktor asked Kathryn," Do you remember our castle from four years ago?"

"Of course, I want to go back some time. Mom tells me that we might visit in a few years with our whole family." She turned to Jacob.

"Would you like that, I mean, us getting all together again, at your place?"

Jacob turned a little red when she had singled him out. "Of course, all of you have to come. We have so much room in the castle."

Kathryn turned to Nathan. "Do you still play piano?"

"Not only piano, but also violin."

"He's very good on both," said Viktor. "We are really proud of him. He's won several prizes at competitions. August is also very talented." He looked at August who just stared at Kathryn. August simply ignored his father. Then, turning to the girl, Viktor asked, "Kathryn, do you still like to sing?"

"Yes, of course," she answered. "Maybe we can do some music together at our home. You know, we have a nice piano. We could play some American folk songs."

"That would be great," said Nathan. "We could also teach you German songs. Right, Jacob?"

"Count me out. I'd rather listen."

Kathryn clapped her hands."That would be so neat!" Then she turned to August. "So, you like music too, August?"

That woke up the tongue-tied young man. "I love music, but I can't speak English so good. I could teach you some nice Austrian songs." He had started to speak English, but soon slipped into his native German. "I also know some great Gypsy melodies and I can play some of them on your piano." He was sorry that there was no piano at the Brenners' house. He had seen the upright piano in the corner of the Carltons' living room.

Jacob felt a little left out of the conversation. Though he was sure of Kathryn's devotion to him, he knew that love of music was one topic they did not share.

Heidi understood that Kathryn tried hard to interest all three boys in her. Though she had her hands full with caring for her two younger children, five-year-old Gretchen and little Hansi who was slightly autistic, she was concerned about her oldest. She decided that an interesting movie might be an activity to interest all four young people. She asked, "We have a great show running right now in our theaters. Have you boys seen your countryman Arnold Schwarzenegger in the movie *Terminator?*"

Here Viktor intervened. "All our boys have seen it. It ran for many months in Graz. You know, 'The Arnold' as we call him, was born in Thal, not far from Graz. We all are very proud of him. It's about an hour's drive from the castle. We hear that they made a sequel, *Terminator 2: Judgment Day.* It came out just before we left. Too bad we couldn't see it."

"Well, "said Richard. "It's running here now. Looks like you are in for a treat. If you'd like to go, I'll get tickets. How about the ladies? Heidi?"

"You know better than asking me, Rich. I prefer staying home with Gretchen and Hansi. How about you, Kathryn?"

"I'll go for sure. I adore that strong guy."

"So, let's see, we need six tickets? How about Grandpa and Grandma?"

"Grandpa Hans, yes; Grandma Erma, no," decided Kathryn. She knew the tastes of her grandparents.

"Seven tickets then. Now we can repay your generous invitation to the opera in Vienna, Viktor."

Viktor looked pleased. "No repay necessary, but we gladly accept your generous offer. So, boys, now you will see your hero, fresh from Hollywood."

Everyone smiled. Heidi offered, "Let's do it tomorrow afternoon. When you come home from that revolting movie, I'll have a nice picnic ready and Grandma Erma will come over to our house."

Richard asked, "Did you say 'revolting?' Better watch your tongue. There are people here who'll love that movie."

Heidi apologized. "Sorry, I should've said 'interesting.'"

Erma intervened. "Don't mind Heidi. I'm on her side. But I know. We are the minority here. So, don't mind us." Then she added. "But you'll appreciate a good meal after the show, anyway." That soothed the ruffled feathers. Needless to say, the movie was a success.

They also visited Springlake in the mountains and met some of the old storytelling friends at the lake. First Kathryn took her friends to their neighbors, the Fosters. Fay and Bob were delighted to see them. "Look how much you've grown, Jacob and Nathan! Well, it's been six years, hasn't it? And that must be August. Erma has told me all about you. You know, Kathy, your grandmother is so excited about this reunion in four years. You have to tell me all about Mary. Erma told us that Luther passed away. We are so sorry about that. Can I offer you something?"

Kathryn had a hard time interrupting Fay. "Sorry, Fay, we can't stay, just wanted to say hello. Are you planning to come to Austria, for the big reunion?"

"No, dear, we are getting too old. I'll help Jean and Ellen to send the invitations, but we just have to wait till everybody comes back and tells us all about it. And be sure to take lots of pictures. You know, Bob really isn't feeling that well anymore. I think that your grandparents won't go either. Austria just is too far away. And your Grandma Erma is five years older than I. Your Grandpa Hans isn't a spring chicken either anymore. So, we'll let you young people go. Well, I see, you're getting antsy. Go along and show your friends around."

Kathryn thanked the two nice old people. "Guess we'll do that. Nice to see you again. So long."

"Thanks for the visit. And come back any time."

The Fosters observed the young people head toward her neighbor's cabin. "What delightful youngsters!" Fay said to Bob. "And don't those boys look smart in their *Lederhosen!* Don't you wish you were their age again, Bob?" said Fay.

"I'm quite happy where I am right now, my dear. Just watching all that energy makes one tired," answered Bob, lowering himself into his comfortable chair.

Nathan and Jacob wanted to see their old home, the Fromms' cabin. There were new people now and even teenagers at that little house. After introducing her friends, Kathryn asked if there was still storytelling going on. "Oh yes, but not in homes at the lake anymore; it's now at the library in Springlake. Every month people come from all over to our library and listen to selected speakers. Maybe you could attend one of those meetings?" Like the Fosters, the new owners wanted to know how the Fromms were doing in Austria and were sorry to hear that Luther had passed away. They had known the Fromms before they had bought their cabin. Kathryn told them that they had to move on and visit other Lake Dwellers. Many of them remembered the two Goldstein boys who had left California in 1985. They got acquainted with August and loved seeing the four young people together. Kathryn proudly led her three friends around the lake. She pointed out the different cabins and told about their owners. The small foot path between the lake shore and the front yards of the cabins led past the wide beach in front of the lodge, crowded with bathers, to a small strip of sand between the lake and a little cabin. Kathryn told the boys, "That's where the mother of one of our friends used to live, her name is Lily and she got married to another Lake Dweller, Gordon Newman. The Newmans live now in Rivertown. They have two little girls, twins, Lexy and Carly, same age as Gretchen. We had storytelling at this house when I almost drowned. I was two then," she explained. "I hadn't learned to swim."

"So, that's when Jacob became your knight in shining armor," August said. *A little cynically*, Jacob thought. *Is he jealous of me?*

"Maybe without him yelling to the others I wouldn't be here," Kathryn said, looking fondly at her former rescuer.

"How come *you* didn't see her in the water?" August asked Nathan who was listening to a bird trilling in the bushes.

"Guess I wasn't into girls then," was the laconic answer.

"Figures," Kathryn threw in. Then she looked at Jacob. "And you were?"

Jacob blushed a little.

"Oh, he doesn't want to tell us," mocked Nathan.

Nathan and August looked at each other and laughed. Both had heard the story about Jacob, the hero, a little too often and were getting tired of listening to it for the umpteenth time.

"What else is there to see at your famous lake?" August wanted to know.

"I'll show you. Now we'll see Aunt Lotti's and Uncle George's cabin. It's really neat." They bypassed the huge estate of Jean and Ellen Dubois and Kathryn told her friends that the owners of the castle-like house were gone for the summer. "They travel a lot. They are very rich and don't have kids. When they are here, they sometimes give huge parties. They are really nice people." Kathryn did not mention Jean's grown-up daughter, Jeannie. She hardly knew the actress who was seldom with her parents.

August was in awe. "It looks like a castle. I thought you didn't have castles in America."

"Not old ones like you have in Austria," said Kathryn. "But there is a famous castle south of here on the coast. My family went there last year and we took the tour of all the rooms. Wow, what a castle."

"I heard of that one," said Nathan. "It's called Hearst Castle and it was built by a rich newspaper man. My father wanted to take us there, but then he died."

They had started on the winding road that led up to the Updikes' cabin. After about half an hour climbing up the steep switchbacks, they reached the parking lot and followed the narrow foot path to the cabin. Lotti was home and happy to see the four young people. "What a nice surprise! You should have let us know and I could have baked a nice coffee cake for you. Now I have only some lemon juice to offer." She led them to the patio and they admired the beautiful view of the blue lake surrounded by houses and trees. A little tinge of fall was in the air.

They settled down on the wooden benches around the picnic table, looking forward to the promised cool drink.

George joined them after a while. He had given swimming lessons all day and was still in his swim trunks, a colorful beach towel slung around his shoulders. The boys were very impressed by his muscular built and his vigorous presence.

He beamed at the four visitors. "Welcome to our home. Thanks, Kathy, for dragging your friends up the hill to see us. So," looking at August, "you are the real Austrian we heard so much about. Lotti told me all about you four years ago. That was quite a surprise story."

August felt a little shy. He liked Lotti's athletic husband, but did not like being singled out. He didn't say anything.

Kathryn took over. "Cat's got your tongue?" then turning to George, "August is just learning English. But," turning to August, "George knows a little German from always being with my grandparents." Then, addressing George, "He never talks much at our home, either."

"Now Kathryn, don't make him feel embarrassed," Lotti intervened. She had come back from the kitchen carrying a tray with glasses of lemon juice. "Tell me, Jacob, how does it feel to be back on your old turf after so many years?"

"Just fine. Nothing has changed much. Or has it, Nathan?"

"No, not much," Nathan agreed. "Only that now there is a new library in Springlake. I hear they even have a Steinway grand piano and that there are concerts and shows given."

"Yes, of course. Thanks to the Duboises, Springlake now attracts people from all over."

The conversation drifted to the events in 1985.

George asked August, "Of course, you heard about those four weddings right here in Springlake?"

"Not really, I know about Viktor and Betty's wedding and of yours. Who were the other couples?"

Kathryn interrupted. "I told you on the way up about that rich couple in the big house by the lake. They are Jean and Ellen Dubois. The fourth couple are the people I told you about, Lily and Gordon. They live now in Rivertown. They used to have a tiny cabin by the dam. They sold that. Lotti, have you seen them lately?"

"Not lately. I think you see them more often than we do. Aren't you friends with the twins?"

"Gretchen is. They are the same age."

"Why don't you visit them on the way back to Oakland," suggested George.

"Yes, why don't you," said Lotti. "You boys must remember the Newmans. The people who took all the pictures at the wedding party."

"Oh yes," Jacob remembered. "The newspaper people. Of course, the ones from Rivertown."

"Great-grandparents Rita and Johann used to live there before they died," said Kathryn. "And Lotti took care of them."

"Right," said George. "You should visit the Newmans on your way home to Oakland. Their twin girls are the age of your sister, Liesl."

"And of my sister Gretchen," added Kathryn. "They plan to come to our big reunion in 1995, and those twins, Carly and Lexy, can hardly wait to meet Liesl then."

August had listened carefully. "Liesl would like to meet those girls."

Lotti smiled. "Sure, she would. I'll call Lily so they know you're coming."

When the evening sun made long shadows over the deck, Kathryn felt that it was time to leave. Her parents, who were staying this weekend at the cabin, must be waiting for them. It was close to dinner time.

Lotti embraced her niece and her three friends and George shook their hands.

"Your Grandma has invited us over for tomorrow for barbecue. Grandpa Hans will make his famous spareribs. It'll be great to see all of you again." Lotti and George accompanied them to the parking lot and returned to their house. Twenty minutes later the four hikers were back at the lake and followed the footpath to the Brenners' cabin.

"Hello, anybody home?" They found the older folks on the deck, enjoying the cool evening breeze. Gretchen and Hansi were playing at the creek, making little floats out of sticks and leaves and watching them be carried away by the rushing water.

Hans and Erma had enjoyed having Viktor all for themselves and hadn't even missed the young people.

On the way back to Oakland the Brenners and the Carltons stopped at the residence of the Newmans in Rivertown and August got acquainted with Gordon, Lily and Gretchen's friends, the twins Carly and Lexy. "Guess what," Gretchen told her friends, "August has a sister in Austria. Her name is Liesl and she is five, just like us."

"Can we see her?" asked Carly.

"You have to come to Austria," August suggested.

"You'll see her in four years at the big reunion." Kathryn said.

"But that's a long time," little Lexy said. "Let's go this summer."

Lily assured the twins that summer was soon over and that they would be too small now to go so far away, but that they would have a great time meeting Liesl in four years. They had been asked by the Duboises to save the June date for that big party in 1995 and to be ready to travel to Austria.

Gordon, whose paper covered the social events in his district, asked if they would mind if he took a few pictures and wrote a little column for his newspaper. Nobody minded. The visitors found it exciting to appear on the news. They even designed a headline for the article:

Native Austrians visit California

"Jacob and I aren't really "native Austrians," objected Nathan.

"That's okay, don't be so fussy! At least all you boys look Austrian in your *Lederhosen.*" Gordon was looking forward to publishing his story in next week's edition of the *Riverside Daily News.*

After an hours' stay at the Newmans the Brenners took their guests back to Oakland. The Carltons stayed a little longer so the girls could catch up on the latest news. All three five-year-olds would start school in the fall. There was so much to talk about!

* * *

The three teenagers from Austria were intrigued by vivacious ten-year-old Kathryn who seemingly had no preference, but had picked Jacob as her favorite playmate. She always felt safe and comfortable with him. Nathan was so studious and August so strange. However, if she had been asked right after the arrival of the boys whom she favored—she wouldn't have picked her good old friend, chubby, jovial, warm-hearted Jacob, nor brilliant-minded Nathan, but dashing, good-looking August. And after a while, her mother became concerned. She thought that August could be dangerous. She didn't know much about him. She felt like protecting Kathryn from August. *Must be that Gypsy blood in him,* she thought to herself. What Heidi did not know about August, can be told in a few paragraphs.

August stood out in the triumvirate. His athletic body, keen features, quick mind, and sheer physical strength attracted people's attention wherever he went. However, he felt insecure because he knew that people were talking about him behind his back. The more August told himself that it was not his fault that his unhappy mother had never been married to his father, the less he felt happy with himself. He felt that he did not belong to the castle people and several times already he had tried to leave but could not do it. He was still so young and had no real education. His mother had never been able to plan for his future, and he had finished elementary school without a goal of what he wanted to pursue in life.

When he had come to Blauenwald in 1987, he was old enough to be accepted at the village middle school, but had not passed the exam to enter. It was not that he wasn't bright enough, but his education so far had been spotty and he had often taken to daydreaming. However, he knew how to read and write and to do some simple arithmetic. But that was all. He had a talent for arts and crafts, but those were subjects that had not been offered in Pristina Polje Elementary School. He had picked up those skills while watching other performers. He had learned by observing other Romas putting on shows and inventing his own style. He was a self-taught artist and he got by with it. Even in the school in Blauenwald singing and dancing, subjects he was good at, were only taught on Saturdays. Only the most talented pupils such as Nathan, were offered private lessons by a professional musician who came twice a week from Graz. August, who never learned to read music, did not qualify for those lessons. However, Mary Fromm, who liked the boy, had taught him rudiments of piano playing.

Back in Kosovo he had been mocked often by the other students, even boys from his own tribe, because he did not have a father. He became very sensitive about this topic. His usual placid expression could change quickly to wild wrath, which scared people. Other young people his age were afraid of him. He was ill equipped to succeed with the exam at the school in Blauenwald. His German was acceptable, though he had mostly conversed with his mother in Romany and had only spoken German in school. He failed the exam for the seventh form—the first year of middle school—where he should have been according to his age and he was put into the sixth and uppermost form of the Blauenwald Elementary School. August's expression tended to be shadowed by a tragic cloud. He preferred being by himself.

Nathan, ten years old when he came to Austria, had had no problems with the exam to enter the highest form of middle school and was an excellent student. He would enter high school in Leibnitz as soon as he graduated from middle school and use his bike for transportation. He did not have to go to Graz like his father since Leibnitz now had its own high school. He had learned the language quickly and was soon at the top of his class. But, like August, he tended to be a loner.

Jacob, different from his brother in so many ways, had a hard time keeping up with his classmates academically and his mother was worried that he might be set back to repeat the class at the end of the school year. School was not Jacob's favorite pastime. Unlike his brother and stepbrother, he preferred roaming around the vineyards and fields, the stables, and the fishpond. When Viktor noticed that Jacob's grades in his academic subjects were sliding, he became concerned and sent the boy to a private teacher. Also Betty was alarmed and helped Jacob with his school work. Soon Jacob caught up and by the end of the school year he was promoted to the sixth form. However, while August and Nathan did not have many friends, Jacob was popular with most everybody. He had an open smile and a pleasant personality that charmed people around him.

Now, in 1991, the difference between the three boys was even more marked. Heidi thought that she detected a certain wildness in August. She noticed that Kathryn was attracted to him and she felt uneasy about this. While both Goldstein boys were like family to her, August was a stranger. Heidi tried to warn her daughter. "Don't become too familiar with boys," she told her. "Boys don't like girls to run after them."

Kathryn thought that her mother was old-fashioned. Boys would always run after girls. Girls could do with boys what they wanted. But she would consider what her mother told her. After all, Mother was older and wiser and she and Dad had a great marriage.

One thing made Kathryn curious. Though August was without doubt a great looking guy and all her female friends agreed with that and were jealous of her; why did he often look so sad? Roly-poly Jacob, not very tall, not very elegant, was always happy. He usually had a sunny smile on his pudgy face. He was a sturdy young man, obviously sure of himself and never brooding like August. Nathan also seemed happy with himself, tall and lank, moving slowly and elegantly, often humming to himself and always politely listening to what others had to say. He seemed to know many things and was anxious to learn more. August had a gloomy expression, tended to argue, and to make himself unpopular. Her girlfriends, smitten by August's good looks, soon found out that he had a streak of haughtiness and tended to make them feel inferior. Truthfully, he felt out of place and by acting arrogantly he thought to defend his low feelings. He never forgot that he was born out of wedlock. A bastard!

The allotted three weeks flew by fast. The boys met most of Kathryn's friends from school, girls as well as boys. They were invited to many different houses and various parties. They saw more movies and even a theater production at the Berkeley University.

Reluctantly, Kathryn did follow her mother's advice. She tried to dole out her favors in equal amounts to the three young men who soon found enough distractions in Oakland and Springlake to keep them busy during the stay in California. Five-year-old Gretchen and little Hansi trotted along with them. After the Baumeisters returned to Austria, they kept up the relations by writing letters. And so, four more years passed by and it was time to get ready for the big ten-year reunion of the Lake Dwellers, plans hatched since 1985. All of Blauenwald was looking forward to the event.

Viktor had become the acknowledged head of the Blauenwald community. Wherever he went, people greeted him respectfully. He had achieved one of his goals. Betty's quiet and friendly demeanor and the fact that both of them were raising their four children responsibly, contributed to the people's acceptance of their castle owner.

But, unfortunately, August's relationship with his father had not improved. That had been Viktor's other goal.

BOOK FOUR

1995-1996

CHAPTER 14

Reunion

The rich couple from Springlake, Jean and Ellen Dubois, had done most of the planning for the ten-year reunion, slated for June 24, 1995. It had been their idea to get the Lake Dwellers together again after ten years of the quadruple wedding in 1985. Early on it had been decided that this reunion should take place in Austria and preparations were going on for months.

It was April now and soon the big gathering would take place. The Baumeisters got excited. Lotti and George Updike had already arrived in Kitzbühl where they found the ski season still in full swing. They would ski as long as snow conditions allowed and then go hiking in the Alps. Right after the reunion in Blauenwald George would fly back to California where his job as swim instructor was waiting. Lotti planned to stay longer and even to travel with her family to southern Germany. The Carltons would come right after the last day of school in the middle of June and would stay in Austria for two months. It would be a well-earned vacation for them. Peter, now twenty-eight and working as a high school teacher in Oakland, married since 1993 and having a small child, was planning to join his older sister when traveling to Austria. His wife did not want to go—she thought that the baby was too young to travel. The parents, Hans and Erma Brenner, also had decided that they would not go to Austria. They felt that they were getting too old. Erma was looking forward to being with her new grandson often and not missing a moment of his growing up. Besides, Hans and she had visited the castle in 1987 and found that that was enough. Like the Fosters, they were not getting any younger. The Newmans from Riverside had planned to stay for a few days at a hotel in Blauenwald Village and then, after the reunion, to do some traveling in Europe.

Other friends could only stay for the weekend of the reunion, while still others planned to stay for several weeks. Jeannie Dubois, Jean's only child, now a well-known movie actress, promised to come, but just for the reunion. She was busy filming a show together with Arnold Schwarzenegger, Austria's native son, the star of the popular *Terminator* sequels. This actor and muscle-builder, born and raised near Graz in the small town of Thal, had made a name for himself by winning several sports contests, moving to America in the late 1960s, starting a successful movie career with *Pumping Iron,* and the less popular *Conan,* and marrying a Kennedy lady. He was scheduled to shoot scenes in a German movie at the time of the reunion. So it wasn't far and it would be easy for Jeannie to get the day off. Her father, the rich oilman and her stepmother Ellen, born McGregor, would be thrilled to see her at the ceremony.

All during spring preparations were underway for the reunion. Jean and Ellen, having the money that was necessary, had promised to arrange the event and they started planning early in the year. After much debate about where to celebrate, it was decided that Viktor's castle was the right place to hold the big party. The affluent couple even had a runway built close to the castle for their private plane. As in 1985 Bob and Fay Foster were instrumental in contacting all the original members of the Springlake Storyteller Circle and "foster" the excitement. They themselves decided not to come the long way to Austria. Bob was not feeling well and, besides, they were not the traveling type. But they did everything possible to help the Duboises make the reunion happen.

Jean and Ellen flew to the castle in January of 1995 and were amazed to meet the extended family of the Baumeisters. They had not seen Viktor and Betty for ten years, though they had corresponded frequently. They had received pictures of the castle, the lovely surroundings, of Viktor and Betty, their children, and the Fromms. But now they met one and all in person and were delighted by what they saw. They walked through the castle grounds and the village and planned for the giant event. The staff at the castle and the villagers admired the vivacious couple, so much more matching their image of Americans than simple Betty had ten years ago.

When also, just a day before the reunion, Jean's actress daughter Jeannie came over from Munich where she had the lead role in a German movie, *Das Mauerblümchen* (The Wallflower) opposite to the Austrian idol, Schwarzenegger, in her elegant private plane (the runway her parents had constructed was useful for her, too), the amazement was reaching the uppermost height and now everyone in Blauenwald was looking forward to the next day when the big celebration would take place.

It had taken all the skillful organizational talents of everyone involved to prepare for the event. Jean Dubois and Fay Foster had been in constant phone connection about the state of the affair. Fay had made the list of participating Lake Dwellers. Besides the five Carltons, Peter Brenner, Lotti and George Updike, Gordon and Lily Newman with their nine-year-old twins, and the two Berkeley teachers, Dr. and Gisela Warner, were willing to participate. There had been flights to be booked, rooms to be reserved, and provisions for meals to be made because Jean and Ellen did not want to burden the castle owners with all the details and finances such a party would affect.

It was a good thing that the Americans arrived at different times before the reunion; some spending extended time before, and others after June 24.

Just as the Brenners gentle neighbor Luise Gilmann had helped the Brenners to get to the airport ten years ago, she did so again and also refreshed Peter's and Lotti's language skills by speaking German to them, which would come in handy while brother and sister were in Austria. Peter did not want to make the same mistake he had committed in 1987 when his knowledge of the German language had been minimal and he had offended the castle staff. He was a willing learner this time and Luise a patient teacher. *She* decided not to go, since she was involved in charity projects and could not afford the time or the money.

Some of the older Lake Dwellers had passed away: Ellen's mother Lucinda, the vigorous lady already an octogenarian in 1985, Esther Silverman, mother of Lily Newman, and Anna Gilmann, Luise's grandmother. In Austria Luther Fromm had died in 1991. Mary

Fromm was getting on in age and *Frau* Grete Schwarz, now almost ninety-five, topped them all and was admired by everyone for her culinary talents and refusal to quit her job as lord of the castle kitchen. Several friends and dignitaries from Blauenwald Village were invited also.

At the beginning of June the first guests arrived. The Carltons would see the castle for the first time, except Kathryn who had gone with the Brenners in 1987. Kathryn was now a young lady of fourteen, still rambunctious and self-centered, and fully aware of her power to attract young men. She was planning to thoroughly enjoy this trip. She looked forward to seeing her Jacob again. Would she still be his only girl? Heidi, who took her shopping, became worried about her daughter's buying frenzies. She warned Kathryn not to accumulate too many things, so that they wouldn't have too much luggage. "One suitcase for you, young lady, that's it. Gretchen and Hansi are only taking what's in their back packs," was the strict order.

"But Mother, I need to pack things for going out, staying at the castle, roughing it and, as you always tell me, enough underwear and night stuff. That doesn't even include shoes. I need everyday shoes, sandals, hiking boots, elegant shoes for Vienna and house shoes. One suitcase just isn't enough."

"Maybe you have to think again. One suitcase for everything and that's it," was Mother's stern reply. "That makes three suitcases for Dad, you, and myself and two back packs for the children. That's plenty."

After a little sullenness Kathryn gave in and the shopping list was cropped until Mother was satisfied. Soon the young lady snapped out of her sullen mood and became her usual lively self again. The big day of the departure arrived sooner than they thought. While Kathryn's younger siblings did not recall the visit of the male Baumeisters in 1991 too well and did not know Mary Fromm, Betty, and Liesl at all, she remembered the entire family quite well and visualized happy times.

The five Carltons arrived first and found the castle bustling with preparations. Kathryn and Jacob fell into each others' arms and were sure that they were meant for each other. In the evening he took his girl aside and told her, "Kathy, I had time to go out with other girls. I tried to forget you. I can't. You are the only one for me and I love you. I want to marry you."

Kathryn looked at him, a little puzzled. "I love you too, Jacob. But isn't it a little early to make wedding plans? You know, I'd like to be with you all my life. But getting married? Let's have our education first. Remember, I'm only fourteen. I'm only getting started in high school this fall. Are you afraid I will date other boys?"

"Who knows what you'll do," he said ominously. "I know it's too early for us to get married. I just wanted you to know how I feel."

"Yes, you grown-up seventeen-year-old," she said mockingly.

"Almost eighteen," he corrected her. His birthday was in July.

"Com'on now, let's enjoy being together. Or," she threatened, "I'll really try out other boys."

"Oh, no," he said, "I'd better act my age." And he gave her a big kiss.

The *Rittersaal* in the castle was ready to hold the American and Austrian guests, which also included Manfred Sattler, the couple Paul and Gerda, the priest Nathanial, and even Raphael who was able to arrange coming over from Rome for the weekend of the reunion party. Also the Blauenwald dignitaries, who would attend Friday's gathering at the *Buschenschank,* were invited to come to the reunion. The Duboises had hired many people from the village to help prepare for the festivities.

On the evening of Friday, June 23, everyone was welcome at the kick-off event at the *Buschenschank* in the village, with many of the villagers attending. It was a joyous party and streams of alcoholic beverages were flowing from the huge barrels in the back of the tavern. The village band was playing and the dance floor was crowded. The mayor of Blauenwald greeted the castle people and their guests and wished them all a good time at their beloved beer tavern. Since Mayor Hausmann spoke a passable English, he addressed the crowd in two languages and everyone applauded him for the effort. The party lasted into the wee morning hours and all went to their respective abodes happily and ready for the celebration at the castle tomorrow.

At two o'clock in the afternoon of Saturday, June 24, the *Rittersaal* began to fill up with the castle people and their guests. The colorful crowd admired the beautiful decorations all around and the tables, laden with tempting foods, arranged alongside the walls. A hired band was playing and the people gathered in the middle of the large room, embracing each other, and sharing happy memories. Everybody wanted to know how the others were doing and the steady murmur of excited partiers was only topped by the cheerful background music of the band.

At one point Viktor clapped his hands and asked the audience's attention. He held a little speech, welcoming his guests and thanking them for coming from far away places to help create this great event. He especially gave thanks to the Duboises and the Fosters who had put the entire event together. In a few words he told the guests about the main happenings at the castle during the last ten years and wished that they would enjoy their stay in his beautiful country. Then he introduced his stepson Nathan, well remembered by the Lake Dwellers, who was now studying music at the Academy for the Fine Arts in Vienna. Nathan played a classical violin selection from Dvorak's beloved *All World Symphony.* The Americans loved the spicy, invigorating folk tunes by the great Hungarian composer. Even August, well versed in Gypsy music, loved to listen to his stepbrother's skillful performance.

Then Paul who, besides his other accomplishments, had a talent for electronics and had rigged up a large TV screen above the podium in the *Rittersaal*, asked for a little more patience and motioned to Gordon Newman, the journalist, to present his picture show of the quadruple wedding ten years ago in Springlake. He and his wife Lily had put together a wonderful slideshow that the Americans as well as the Austrians very much enjoyed.

"Look! That was the big moment!" People nudged each other when the four happy couples stood together in their wedding outfits, looking so young and expecting nothing but bliss of the future. All four of those couples were present, the Duboises, the Newmans, the

Updikes, and the proud castle owners, the Baumeisters, now surrounded by their offspring.

"What a memorable party!"

"Let's take a lot of pictures this time, too."

This was the clue for Gordon and Lily to ask the guests to group together for picture taking and many formal and candid shots were taken. The Newman couple promised copies to everyone.

It was Paul's idea to take a picture of the four original couples with their children. That group picture turned out well and it was added to the gallery of ancestors in the castle library. Here the fifteen people: the Baumeisters with their four children of varied descent, the Newmans with the twins, the Duboises with Jeannie, and George and Lotti, smiled down on relatives, friends, and visitors to remind them of the great event in 1995.

During the buffet style meal—aided by the excited castle staff, flitting back and forth among the partiers, offering drinks and plates with assorted delicacies—the band played lovely national music and even some American favorites like *Saturday Night Fever* and for the older folks, *Lawrence Welk Melodies.*

The pinnacle of the evening was a little drama concocted only the evening before by Jeannie Dubois and August, featuring highlights from the wedding party in 1985 enacted by both talented performers. August also did some of his dancing skits that he had done in Kosovo to help earn his and his mother's living. The actress and the dancer put on such a delightful program that all the people were enthralled. Memories flooded back and people loved to see themselves as they were ten years ago.

Another performance gripped the partiers. Four beautiful nine-year-old girls, all of them lithe and willowy, dressed in chiffon gowns of four different pastel hues, danced a May dance to the tune of a German folksong, played by Nathan. They were Liesl, Gretchen, and the Newman twin girls. It had been their own idea and they had practiced with Nathan for several days before the party.

Gordon and Lily bustled around to catch every moment on their cameras to be sent out to all participants after they were at their homes again and wanted to relive the reunion.

Viktor had encouraged others to come forward and share their memories with everyone and some of them did. Ellen and Jean told the crowd how happy and busy they had been and how they had enjoyed preparing for this party. George and Lotti, both of them radiating energy and happiness, told about their interesting lives as mountain people, working together as a team: she as a nurse, and he as the swimming and ski instructor at Springlake and other mountain resorts in California. Even Jeannie took the stage to do a little speech, accompanied by vivid gestures and interesting tales about her life in the spotlight. She was now the lead in a German movie series featuring the native Austrian star Arnold Schwarzenegger. Her role in this movie was depicting the "rags to riches" life of an inconspicuous girl from a poor background intriguing a flashy sports tycoon. The Austrians were very proud of their now famous countryman. Though his newest role in the film series *Conan* had threatened to undermine his reputation, everyone was interested in Arnold's move to the United States, marrying a Kennedy lady, producing a wonderful family of four children, and starting the popular series *Batman and Robin.* Too bad that the famous actor had politely declined to follow an invitation to the reunion. But everyone was happy that at least Jeannie could be with them.

A few weeks before his death in 1991 Luther Fromm had predicted that Arnold Schwarzenegger might become famous in politics also.

Nathan had added, "Maybe he could be the president of the United States?"

Luther had thrown cold water unto this. "Unfortunately, his European birth would prevent that."

"How about Arnold becoming the governor of California?" Viktor had suggested. "Now, that's a possibility," Luther had agreed. Mary had her own thoughts. *My dear husband; how long will we still have him in our midst?* And then it had happened. Luther had joined Rudolf and Maria in the family vault.

Peter, who loved being the center of attention, had prepared a humorous report about their trip to Vienna and the discovery of their stepbrother. Skillfully he steered away from the sensitive parts of this and turned the shocking event into an interesting drama. He motioned to August to tell about this himself. August, resenting this a bit, had no choice but taking the stage and he told the audience about his life in Kosovo and the sad event of his mother's death, which brought tears to many eyes. Viktor and Betty were not so sure about August's feelings, but were thankful that nothing seemed to taint the good spirit of the party. One of the last speakers was *Frau* Grete Schwarz who spoke slowly so that the Americans could understand her. Nobody in this big room had lived so long as she. She told the audience that the *Spuk* would be quiet from now on. Little Liesl and the Carltons' youngest, Hansi, the autistic boy who had found a wonderful friend in the gentle girl, had followed adventurous Kathryn who *had* to investigate the mysterious attic above the east wing. Just on top of *Frau* Grete's room a group of rats had ensconced themselves and had made a racket there for many years. That was the *Spuk* and after thoroughly cleaning the attic, throwing out the trash, and closing all holes to the outside, no more noise would ever be heard. *Frau* Grete assured the folks that now the attic was thoroughly *aufgeräumt* and disinfected. For years she had not been able to climb up that rickety ladder into the attic, but now she delegated the task to younger helpers and saw to it that everything stayed under control. In fact, the strong odor of ammonia was drifting through cracks of ceilings to all the rooms in the east wing.

"Good," Betty whispered to Viktor, "that's finally solved. Now our castle can go on being respectable again. Unless somebody else settles on top of Grete's room."

The last speaker was Raphael who came wearing his red travel alb worn by cardinals on secular occasions. He told the gaping crowd about life at the Vatican and his satisfaction that all seemed to go well at his previous work place in Austria.

The folk tunes changed to dance music and the rest of the evening was danced away by the light of the moon, shining through the tall windows of the *Rittersaal.*

On Sunday everyone slept in. Breakfast was a lonely affair, attended only by Viktor and Betty, who supervised the cleanup after the big party. *Frau* Grete, who had much to do in her kitchen, and

Sepp Wanz, who felt that someone ought to supervise the tending of the livestock, had their breakfast together in the dining room by the kitchen.

"Well, some party, I should say." Sepp enjoyed the spicy omelet that *Frau* Grete had served him.

"Oh yes, wasn't it wonderful to have the old castle so busy with all these people. Do you remember, Sepp, how lonesome it felt after the old Baumeisters had died so suddenly?'

"It sure did feel lonesome. I hope that Master Viktor and Mistress Betty will be around for a long time. By the way, don't you hit ninety soon? Didn't you come to the castle in the early '20s?"

"Sure did, I was barely twenty when I started with old Master Rudolf in '22. I'll never forget those early years. I hit ninety four years ago."

"Really! Missed another occasion for a party."

"Not for the likes of me, Sepp."

"Don't say that. The castle wouldn't be what it is now without you, Grete."

"If you say so. You're just trying to butter me up."

She poured another cup of coffee for both of them. It was nice to feel so important.

On Monday some of the guests had to leave. The Warners left for their beloved Dresden. The Newmans had to go back to their newspaper business. George Updike was needed at Springlake. And the Duboises had travel plans around the globe. The rest of the people enjoyed their stay and did various trips to the surroundings, to Graz, and to Vienna. One big outing was planned for the next weekend to Lake Neusiedl on the border between Austria and Hungary.

CHAPTER 15

Neusiedl Lake, Revenge

August, whose relationship with his father had not improved one iota during all the years he was living in the castle, was still brooding about a way to hurt Viktor deeply. He wanted revenge for the way Viktor had treated his mother. He managed to have a revealing talk with Peter Brenner who, so August had noticed, liked to talk about any topic and who seemed to know more than anybody around the castle. Of course, there was always *Frau* Grete, but August thought that she was too preoccupied with her mystical intuitions. Besides, he liked Peter. He was not to be disappointed.

The two young men were walking together in the spruce forest, when August asked Peter, "Would you know things from Viktor's past, or about his ancestors?"

This was Peter's element. "What would you like to know, August?"

"Some juicy gossip perhaps?"

"There would be some of that, but why do you want to know?"

"Never mind, Peter, just curious. I only know those reverent ancestors by name and by the pictures hanging in Viktor's study and the library. Not much to learn from that."

"Well, I know some. You see, I was a teenager when everybody around our lake in California told stories. Viktor told us about his grandfather and how he and his mistress—sorry, wrong word—his future wife had this baby, Viktor's Uncle Karl, (actually half-uncle) *before* they got married. I wanted to know more about that but my mother shut Viktor up because there were young children around, meaning, of course those two Goldstein boys, your stepbrothers. So, that's all the juice from that story. Is that what you wanted to hear?"

August let this information ferment in his mind. Then he said, "Peter, you could do me a great favor. As you say, *Frau* Grete has been at the castle longer than anyone else here. Maybe she remembers about those times before Rudolf and Maria married. You seem to get along so well with *Frau* Grete. She might tell you some more about this "scandal.""

"I'll see what I can do, August. You certainly whet my interest."

Frau Grete was only too ready to have a good chat with Master Peter and invited him to sit down with her at her desk while her helpers were busy cutting vegetables for *Mittagessen*. After complimenting him on his improved knowledge of German and presenting some tea and cake in front of him, she asked him what he wanted to know.

"Do you remember our conversation when my family visited in 1987?"

"That's a long time ago, Master Peter. Let's see, didn't you want to know about Master Viktor's parents and grandparents?"

"Yes, and you told me that. But I thought there was something not quite right with my Uncle Karl—I thought that Viktor said something about it and my mother shut him up—what could that have been?"

Frau Grete put her hand to her forehead and tried to remember. "So, I never really told you that Master Karl was born before his parents got married?"

"No, you didn't," said Peter. "You just mentioned that Rudolf and Maria had two sons, Alfred and Karl. But when Viktor told us about his castle—I was a teenager then—he mentioned something about Maria being Rudolf's mistress and Karl being born while Rudolf was still married to Alfred's mother. But my mother shut him up because there were young boys around. I'd like to know from you if that was true? You know so much about the people here, more than anybody else in the castle."

Frau Grete loved to be flattered. Nobody around the castle paid that much attention to her stories. She took another sip of tea and cleared her throat.

"So you know that the old Baumeisters worked hard to improve our castle. When they moved in the 20s with their son Karl," she looked around as if to make sure that no one was listening and whispered, "there was a rumor that Karl was born before they got married ..." Peter made a surprised face. "Of course, Master Alfred, the father of our Master Viktor, was the regular son of Master Rudolf and his first wife, Friederike. She died before the old Baumeisters bought the castle." *Frau* Grete spoke so low now that Peter had to lean forward to catch all her words. "There had been things going on between Master Rudolf and *Fräulein* Maria and people in the village were saying that *Frau* Friederike died of grief. All this happened before they bought the castle, when they were still living in Graz. But, you know, people from Blauenwald know people in Graz and they had heard about the scandal. Also the *Spuk* was acting up."

Peter made a horrified face. "Of course, the *Spuk*. You don't say that—"

"Oh yes, Master Peter, Karl was born out of wedlock. It those days, and even today, that's pretty unacceptable. Maybe not so much in America?" she added shyly.

"I guess it would be considered scandalous in America too. What happened then?"

Frau Grete continued. "The war came. Karl became a soldier and was killed in 1945, just before the end of the war. The old parents lived on for several years, keeping Blauenwald up with the help of a manager. I took care of the household.

"After he had finished his studies at Vienna, Alfred worked at the *Weingut* of Manfred Sattler in the neighboring village of Reichenfels. Manfred and his wife Ursula were good friends of Alfred and Susanne Baumeister. They had already been good neighbors to the much older Rudolf and Maria.

"After the death of their son Karl, his old parents never quite recuperated. The war was over in 1945 and they led a quiet life. They didn't even travel anymore. They died, one after another, in the beginning of the 1950's. Both, Rudolf and Maria Baumeister were laid to rest in the family vault outside the castle. The entire community of Blauenwald attended the funeral."

Peter felt that she was getting off the track. "So, to get back to the time when they had Karl, Rudolf was still married to Friederike? Just wanted to make sure I understood you right. And then you got suspicious because the Spuk was so loud?"

"Oh yes, Master Peter. That's what I was telling you. But then Rudolf and Maria got married and the *Spuk* was pretty quiet for a while."

"One more thing, *Frau* Grete. You must know more than anyone here in the castle about what kind of person Karl was. Did he have a lot of girlfriends? Was he different from his brother Alfred?"

He seemed to have hit a raw nerve. "Girlfriends? Oh my, yes. He was a real ladies' guy, just like his father. Dashing young man! People talked about him. He even had a baby somewhere, but it died."

This was Peter's cue to end the conversation. He had learned all he was after. He would be able to tell August all about the juicy rumor, substantiated by a true eyewitness. He was not interested in the rest of *Frau* Grete's account about the legitimate married lives of August's ancestors.

The next day Peter and August met again and Peter related all he had learned to the younger man.

August had heard what he wanted. "That's very interesting. Thank you so much, Peter. So that straight-laced great-grandfather of mine wasn't such a saint after all. I wonder how Karl felt—I mean, being illegitimate. Maybe he didn't even know."

"*Frau* Grete says that Rudolf and Maria were married a short while before they bought the castle. Karl was about four years old then. I don't know if he knew."

"They didn't abandon him?" was August's leading question.

"Of course not, why would they?"

"Just wanted to make sure."

August thought for a while and asked, "When Viktor told that story about the castle, did he mention what kind of a man his grandfather was?"

"Yes, in fact he mentioned that he was a real ladies' man when he was younger. As far as I remember—you know, August, that was about twelve years ago—old Rudolf Baumeister was still married to that rich old noble woman Friederike, when he met Karl's mother and did his thing with her while the poor woman was still alive and in the next room." Peter and August looked at each other knowingly and started to chuckle. Peter continued. "So I heard something then, but not the whole story."

"I get it. Viktor's grandpa wasn't quite the esteemed proper man we children are supposed to fathom about him. Anything juicy about Viktor's parents?"

"Not that I'd know about, really. But your Uncle …forgive me, Granduncle Karl"—Peter was a stickler when it came to relation-ships—"must have done some of those things. At least *Frau* Grete told me so. Why don't you ask Viktor?"

"I'm asking you. I'm not too close to him. Did you ever hear what he did to my mother?"

"*Frau* Grete told me a little when we visited in 1987. Wasn't that a real scandal?"

"So you heard. Yes, he and my mother …," August shrugged his shoulders. "You know why I'm not very happy about that."

Peter looked at the young man and felt sorry for him. "I can un-derstand that." He thought of his own secure home life. No hidden scandals there, everything was in the open.

"Did I answer your questions? Is there anymore you want to know?"

"I wonder how Alfred felt when he heard his mother cry at night when she knew that his father had another woman in *her* bed."

"Probably awful," Peter said. "Anything else?"

"No, thanks. I heard enough already. Let's go home."

On the way home August asked casually, "Your niece looks like a nice girl."

"Yes, she's okay. Has lots of boyfriends. But she wants to marry Jacob, that little squat. He's half a head shorter than she. Girls!" he said, "hard to figure out."

"So she is popular?"

"You bet. Could have anyone she wants to. Now she has three admirers here in Austria."

"And Viktor adores her, too."

"You're right. She is his favorite niece. That's what he calls her. Actually she is a second cousin once removed. There are other relatives from his mother's side, but Kathryn is his favorite." Peter liked to be precise.

August mused. "Wonder what she sees in Jacob."

"Why don't you ask her?"

"You're kidding? She'd kill me."

"Want to bet? She would be honored. Make her forget that short guy."

They had reached the gate, nodded a brief *hallo* to Rupert, and were up the stairs in three big steps. Just in time for *Mittagessen.*

August did not talk during the meal. He had to work on his plan. Just by fate he sat next to Kathryn. She looked at him, as he thought, a little haughtily. So Viktor's grandfather had been doing things in the same vein as his grandson, being careless and inconsiderate and in addition being cruel to his unloved wife. Both men and also "Uncle" Karl had committed atrocities to other people closely bound to them. August pondered this in his disturbed heart. Outwardly he did not show a thing. He had always been fairly distant to the other people, his relatives, as well as the castle staff. But now he felt that he might have inherited some of those base Baumeister genes and he continued to brood.

George Updike had to leave the day after the big party and Lotti would stay with the Carltons and her brother Peter for two more weeks. They would travel in Austria and Germany and they'd fly home together. Quite a large group of people still remained at the castle after most of the other guests had left.

Viktor and Betty had prepared for the big outing to Neusiedl Lake. They had chosen this rather inconspicuous area because they had older and very young people in the group. To go to the popular high mountains would have been more difficult for them. They needed two station wagons, one Viktor's, the other one rented by Richard Carlton. The two nine-year-olds, Liesl Baumeister and

Gretchen Carlton, who sat in the passenger seat in the front of Viktor's car, were happy to be together. Peter and Lotti sat on the two middle seats. Kathryn, sitting close to Jacob in the back, experienced a strange feeling when lanky August squeezed his body next to her, folding his long legs underneath the seat in front of him. The rest of the party sat in Richard's big wagon. Mary had decided that she was too old for this trip and Gerda would take care of her.

It was not very far to Burgenland. By noon both cars had arrived at the Hungarian border and had a *Jause* at a *Buschenschank* in Steinamanger, or, as the Hungarians called it, *Szombathely*. Viktor told his guests that they would have time to visit the old Cathedral. Some ancient buildings from the Roman time were still recognizable—the small town was founded by the emperor Claudius in 45 AD, which makes it the oldest settlement in Hungary. It was interesting for the Americans, as well as the Austrians, to be surrounded by the sounds of the Hungarian language. Peter, while in college, had come across some interesting facts about this strange language, called *Magyar* by the Hungarians. He had even learned some *Magyar* phrases.

He explained to the others, "That language doesn't even belong to the family of Indo-European languages. It is related to Finnish. It's very hard to learn."

They were sitting in a restaurant and were served by a young waiter who asked them something in Hungarian.

"Peter, can you tell him that we don't speak their language?" Rich asked. "Let's see." Peter thought for a minute while the waiter waited patiently.

"Nem értek magyarul beszélek." (We don't speak *Magyar*)

"Aha," said the waiter. "You're Germans?"

"igen (yes)."

Now the waiter spoke German with a Hungarian accent. Peter was truly admired and he loved the attention.

Viktor explained that most people close to the border spoke both languages. Many also were able to converse a little in English.

After the meal, they continued toward Braunegg on the shore of Lake Neusiedl, crossing the border between Hungary and Austria once more. In that little town a friend of Viktor from his study years in Vienna was the owner of the *pension* Storchenblick. Braunegg was a small village, consisting only of a few farms, a store, and the friend's inn. It was governed from Donnershausen, a bigger town nearby. From far they could detect the chimney on top of the house, occupied by a family of storks. The wide nest was filled with the white body of the mother stork, surrounded by several little ones, all chattering with their red beaks. Just in that moment when they arrived at the parking lot of the *pension*, the father stork flew in with food in his beak for his family.

"Look, Mommy, big bird," cried little Hansi, pointing to the top of the chimney. "Yes, Hansi," said Heidi, "see how the Daddy feeds his kids." They all looked at the tender scene and were touched. Only August —never letting off his dark thoughts—told himself: *not even the stork abandons his babies.*

They unpacked and followed their friendly host into the large house, through the friendly lobby into the large hall with a huge oaken dining table, surrounded with wooden benches. Everything was decked out in Austrian décor. The hostess motioned them to climb up the stairs to the many bedrooms on the second floor. Soon they were settled in their rooms and ready to explore their home for the next three days.

"What a nice little family you have on top of your roof," said Lotti to the housewife who was bustling around to make everybody comfortable.

"Yes, the same stork comes every spring and settles here. He likes our chimney because it's so wide and comfortable for him to build his nest. This year he only had to add a few twigs and feathers—the nest was still quite good and wasn't destroyed during the winter storms. We always greet him like an old friend and I think he appreciates that. This year he sure has a nice family."

"Yes," added the host who had listened to their conversation. "He is such a good friend, we even gave him a name: Peter."

"That's my name!" Peter was delighted. Not only the German shepherd at the castle, now also a stork had his name. What a small world!

Viktor asked if there was still time to venture out to the lake, right behind the farmhouse, before the evening meal. "Sure, plenty of time. *Abendbrot* is at eight o'clock. You have almost two hours till then. It's warm enough for a nice swim. Just go through the garden and you'll find the little gate to the beach. Be sure to always close the gate, or we'll have some unwelcome guests. Pelicans love our vegetables."

"Pelicans!"

"Oh, yes, there are hordes of them out there in the reeds. And always hungry."

They were ready in no time to venture out to the lake. They strolled through the garden with rows and rows of vegetables and fruit trees, found the little gate, and the white stretch of sand between two tall patches of reeds. It was a nice, balmy afternoon and the pleasantly warm water invited them for a good swim.

While the younger people were frolicking in the shallow water, and Heidi had taken tired little Hansi to his bed, Betty, Viktor, and Richard sat on their towels, spread over the white sand on the beach and took in the pleasant scene in front of them. The light wind had calmed down and dusk was setting in. The rushes surrounding the lake were rustling quietly and all kinds of birds flew in from the lake's center to settle for the night. A few screeches sounded from the reeds, getting fainter and fainter, until light faded away and the blues and greens of the water turned into a uniform pearl-gray. The last bird still awake was a lonely egret—a white heron—standing on one leg close to their place on the beach. Only the noise of the happy swimmers kept the solitary bird from coming closer to them.

At seven o'clock it was time to gather the troops and get ready for the evening meal. One by one the young people joined the three older ones on the beach. One more look at the beautiful red and orange sky and they returned to the *pension*, Viktor making sure that the little gate was locked.

He looked at his watch. "Just enough time to get ready for supper," he announced. Their friendly hosts had an inviting meal ready on the large dining table in the large hall. There was a terrine of spicy hot soup, a variety of home-baked breads and rolls, including the typical black bread or *Schwarzbrot, Aufschnitt,* such as home-made cheeses and sausages, *Leberwurst* and *Blutwurst* and sliced ham to choose from on big platters. Fresh butter and sour cream were available to spread on the bread. For dessert huge bowls with fresh-picked raspberries were set out, accompanied by solid whipped cream that had the serving spoon standing upright in it.

After the meal, all of them sat together for a while and talked about their plans for the next day. Viktor's friend invited the guests to have a tour of his farm, which had a variety of produce and animals and also grapes. Viktor and Jacob gladly accepted—they were interested to see how farmers in the Burgenland managed their estates. Nathan, Peter and Lotti decided to visit an old church in Donnerskirchen. The older adults, Betty and the Carltons, just wanted to relax and stay at the inn and the beach with the younger children. Kathryn was not intrigued by any of these plans. She wanted to rent a bicycle and ride around the lake. Therefore she was happy when August asked her to come with him. He would get the bikes early in the morning. They all went to bed early. August was amazed how easy it was to get Kathryn away from the two other pursuers.

It was great to wake up to a new surrounding and hear the birds sing, feel the warm sunrays, and smell the comforting odor of freshly brewed coffee. Kathryn was happy to get out into the fresh air. After a refreshing swim at the little stretch of white sand, she was in the mood to venture out. Jacob had not talked much to her since the long drive. He felt a little left out and did not want to appear jealous. August had stayed close to Kathryn and it was obvious that she was not oblivious to his interest in her. Jacob did not like the idea of her being alone with August for several hours and tried to interest her in coming along with him and his father to see the farm. But to no avail—his girl had made up her mind. August had the bikes ready and told Kathryn that they would leave around nine o'clock. Jacob gave up trying to talk sense into her and joined the others who had breakfast in the lobby. At least he had made plans for sailing on the lake in the afternoon and hoped for Kathy to join him then.

Neusiedl Lake was about sixteen kilometers (ten miles) long and four kilometers wide, and there were no obstacles in the surrounding bike path. The hostess assured August, who inquired about the time it would take to ride around the lake.

"You can easily do it in two to three hours. It's a very nice ride."

"We'll be back in about three hours," August told Viktor and after a questioning look to Betty who seemed to approve, he nodded his consent. He felt reluctantly good about the fact that August had taken the pains to consult with him. He told him, "If you leave now, you'll be back in time for *Mittagessen*. We did not plan anything with the group for this afternoon, so you can take your time."

Heidi added, "I hope you take good care of our Kathryn. Don't let her talk you into any silly adventures." She had forgotten about her original suspicious feelings about the young man and thought that now at the age of nineteen they should trust him.

"I'll take good care of her," was August's cryptic answer. *As if she needs my good care,* he thought. Kathryn smiled at August and Jacob felt a strange feeling of jealousy welling up inside of him. He also felt that danger was lurking for her. She shouldn't flirt with him like that. August was such a strange guy. Could he be trusted with his precious girl?

"Be sure to be back for the sailing trip at two this afternoon," he reminded Kathryn. Earlier in the morning the two had arranged to rent a sailboat and Peter who knew about this sport had agreed to go with them.

"Sure, we'll be back by then, most likely much earlier," August assured the others. He had his own plans and sailing on the lake was not one of them.

The hostess had prepared a small package with sandwiches and two bottles of Coke for a little *Jause* and Kathryn put it into the basket in front of her bike.

As planned, around nine o'clock on Friday morning August and Kathryn took off, starting on the narrow bicycle path hugging the reeds surrounding the shallow lake. She had chosen to wear a light summer dress and riding the bike felt almost like flying. During the first hour neither of them spoke much. The birds in the reeds had woken up and a uniform chattering filled the air so that they could not hear each others' voices. When they entered the *Seewinkel* on the south edge of the lake, August motioned to his companion to stop and get off their bikes. Kathryn looked around with wide eyes. "Look, pelicans!" she pointed to a group of the hefty, snow-white birds, standing together, moving their plump, long beaks so it looked like a serious discussion. "Wonder what they are talking about?' she pondered.

"Let's find a nice little place and eat our sandwiches," suggested August, getting ready to set his plan in action. He did not have much experience with girls. The village girls, all too eager to be taken out by the virile young man, were disappointed by his obvious aloofness. Kathryn, with all her joviality and vitality, was after all, an oldest child raised strictly by a caring mother and still so young. Most likely she didn't have much experience either. It seemed foolish of her to trust him so utterly. Would she be of any help, or more likely, would she resist him? Anyway, it didn't matter. His mind was set—it had to be done.

They found a lovely spot, surrounded by reeds, far enough away from the bicycle path so as not to be disturbed by bikers. Kathryn had taken the lunch that their hostess had packed lovingly out of the basket of her bike and August spread the tarp he had stashed on the holder in back of his bike. While they were munching the tasty egg sandwiches and washing them down with Coke from plastic bottles, the world around them became one endless space, filled with the blue of the sky, the green of the reeds, and the grayish waves of the lake, dotted with the white sails of colorful boats. Multitudes of birds around them provided a monotonous concert, only interrupted by occasional trumpet-like sounds of aggressive white pelicans, wooing their females. Oblivious of August's clumsy attempts to make her cooperative, she continued chattering in her girlish way.

"Wait till I tell my friends in school about this. August, did you ever think there could be so many birds? In Oakland we hardly ever see white herons and pelicans. Too many people around. There are only some geese and ducks at Lake Merrit. Oh, this is so beautiful." She stretched out next to the boy who carefully collected the papers and empty bottles of their lunch and put it on the side of the tarp.

Just as carefully he put his arm under Kathryn's neck. With the other hand he fumbled underneath her light summer dress and found her underpants. With one quick grip he ripped them off and threw them aside. This was the moment he had so carefully planned and he was not surprised when Kathryn tried to sit up instantly, alarmed, and terrified.

"August, what are you doing, no, no, don't!"

But the boy was faster than she. Suddenly he turned from admirer to seducer. He became the master. Brutally he covered her mouth so she couldn't scream and forced her to lie down again, helpless now in the crook of his arm. His free hand cleared the way and lifted her dress; he threw himself on top of her, pinned her down and entered her. No gentleness, no careful foreplay, no mercy. The girl writhed and wriggled, terrified and desperate. She felt the full virile force of the boy. She was not prepared for this. She was the victim of rape. Her world was shattered.

August was spent. While she was struggling, he was conquering. It was done. Now he could only see what the consequences were of all of this. If Kathryn became pregnant, he had his revenge. If she did not, he had at least tried. He knew enough about the creation of a new life to be aware of the possibility that his attempt to make Kathryn pregnant might be a failure. He was not even debating the fact that he had committed a serious crime by raping an innocent girl. But he, August, was created this way, so the only way—in his warped mind—was to redeem his pitiful existence the same way. And it had to be someone close to his father. When he regarded the little heap of the crying girl next to him, so proud and strapping just a few minutes ago, he felt nothing but disgust, with himself, with Kathryn, with the world around him. Coldly he threw the discarded clothes at her and ordered her to get dressed and get up. He put the tarp on the back of his bike, the used papers from their lunch into Kathryn's basket, and mounted his bike.

"Let's go, they are waiting for us. We said to be back before one o'clock."

Kathryn got up slowly, straightened out her scanty clothes and looked at the boy casually sitting on his bike and waiting for her.

"You—are a monster. How could you do this to me? Why? What shall I do now?"

"You'll never understand." The boy said with clenched teeth. "It had to be done. You'll get over it. If there should be a child, your parents will take care of you. Viktor did this to my mother. And she had nobody. Do you understand now?"

Kathryn felt like never before. Her whole world had broken down. How could she ever face her parents again? She could only hope that she did not get pregnant. But even then, she had lost her sunny childhood. How could she face Jacob now? Jacob, who had trusted her and would never believe it when she told him what had really happened. And she knew that he wanted to marry her—some day. Who would have known how bitter August's feelings were toward his father?

On the way home neither of them spoke a word. Silently they agreed not to say anything of this to the others yet. They had to play a charade. It would be hard. Both knew—or thought they knew— that it would at least take two months to be sure and that it was then the time to make a decision. Just before they entered their *pension* at Braunegg, August told Kathryn coldly, "If you are pregnant, I don't mind if you have an abortion. If you want the child, have it. I do not want it. Maybe Jacob will forgive you. I am going to enlist in the army. There will be a war in my homeland soon."

So both young people had new lives facing them in the near future. Life would never be the same again for them.

Kathryn was brave enough to go sailing with Jacob and Peter. But in the evening, after the meal, she broke down. She knocked on her parents' door, found her mother by herself, just getting ready for bed. Rich was still downstairs, having a beer with Viktor and Peter. Mother and daughter were together and Heidi heard the grizzly news from her crying daughter. "Oh, mother, what shall I do? It was so awful."

For Heidi this revelation was a blow beyond measure. She, not ever having been raped, dimly felt what her daughter was going through. However, any little rift between her and her daughter suddenly disappeared, and she felt nothing but deepest sympathy. Her daughter had confided in her; that was the only thing that counted. She had to help her. Kathryn needed her full support. There would be enough people criticizing her once the story came out.

"My poor darling; we should have never let you go on this trip. We trusted August, and he has let us all down. We can only do one thing now: wait and see what happens. The others shouldn't know about any of this. It would ruin the rest of our reunion. Tomorrow we have planned the trip to Eisenstadt. Do you think you can go along and pretend nothing has happened?"

"I shall try. It will be hard not to tell Jacob."

"It would be better to wait with that. Jacob would feel terrible about it. He really loves you. Maybe nothing has happened and all will be all right." Heidi was not so sure what *she* would do, if Kathryn was pregnant. One thing was sure; she would always be there for her. In any event she would not talk to her husband now. She would wait till they were back in Oakland and then take her daughter to her own gynecologist. She would make sure that this birth would not take place. Her daughter was too young to shoulder the responsibility of motherhood. Her first grandchild? Well, it was a tragedy and Kathryn's happiness was at stake. She believed that Kathryn had told her the truth about August forcing her. She took her daughter in her arms and thanked her for coming to her.

"Kathryn, my love, I am glad you confided in me. This is as far as it'll go now. We will not let anyone else know. Back at home I'll tell your father and together we'll make decisions."

Kathryn nodded, hugged her mother, and left for her own room. Just then her father came in, happy and contented. "Having a nice little chat with Mommy?" he asked cheerfully. "Sleep well after your full day and be ready for a great day tomorrow."

Kathryn just stared at her father and went to her room.

Heidi tossed and turned for a while, but then sleep took over. In the morning she woke up with a jolt. She remembered how she had felt last night after Kathryn's confession. However, this morning it was different. The weather had changed and Heidi's feelings toward yesterday's events had also changed. She decided to have the problem attacked as soon as possible. She made up her mind to have the doctor in Blauenwald examine Kathryn and take it from there.

Nobody but Heidi Carlton, besides August and Kathryn, knew about the drama that was going on in their midst.

The weather on Saturday was not as nice as Friday. The trip to Eisenstadt was delayed by a rain shower and it was already close to noon when they all left.

August watched Kathryn closely and noticed how tightly she clung to her mother and how serious both of them stayed through-out the trip. He had not slept well. He did not feel that his plan to rape Kathryn and thus to hurt his father had gone well. His father did not even know about it. August had utterly underestimated the girl. Why did she behave so stoically? Why didn't she run around, accusing him of rape? Why did she act so chummy with her mother when before yesterday she had sort of avoided her? August felt that now he was surrounded by enemies. He wished that Raphael was still in Blauenwald. Besides Liesl he was the only person August re-ally felt close to. But Liesl was still too young to understand and the priest was gone. His successor did not even know about August's dilemma. His stepmother? She had her own problems. And Jacob, that milk face? August had no feelings for him. He evidently had no idea and seemed to enjoy the trip thoroughly. Kathryn must not have told him yet. Nathan? He lived in his own world.

Viktor had arranged to visit the Esterhazy castle and gardens. The century old buildings and parks, still occupied by royalty, were now owned by Melinda, the wife of the late Paul V who passed away in 1989. She, once the celebrated prima ballerina at the National Opera Hause, was still alive in 1995, lived in Zürich, and managed the Eisenstadt holdings. Tourists from all over the world visited her. One of the most renowned employees of the Esterhazy's was the musician and composer Josef Haydn who had his own house and church left as legacy. In order to please Nathan, Viktor had planned to attend a concert in the Haydn Music Room in the afternoon. Hei-di, Rich, and Kathryn, sensing that the concert would be too much for the younger children, left the palace after the tour and found a quiet little café in the city where they relaxed with hot chocolate and pastries. The rest of the party enjoyed the concert, strolled through the garden—now a beautiful park with lakes and pavilions, and then joined the Carltons. After the short ride to their farm in Braunegg, all were tired and went to bed. Nobody, except Betty, had noticed anything different about Kathryn and August. Betty thought that it was strange that Kathryn was so quiet and that August behaved moodier than ever. She also noticed that Heidi and Kathryn were closer than before. One more person had noticed the change in Kathryn. That was her Aunt Lotti.

On Sunday, the last day at Neusiedl Lake, nothing was planned but to enjoy the good weather. The rain had ceased and sunshine prevailed throughout the day. Everyone did what he or she pleased. Victor and Betty strolled alongside the lake. The Carltons settled at the beach. Gretchen and Liesl, inseparable like twins, built sand-castles and splashed in the shallow water. Jacob and Nathan rented bikes and explored the neighborhood. August, the loner again, stayed by himself and read a book. Kathryn, unusual for her, remained in her room. She shared this room with Lotti.

She sat on her bed, staring at one point at the wall when Lotti came in quietly and, seeing the far-away look on Kathryn's face, sat down next to her on the bed. Kathryn turned her back on her and Lotti understood that something terrible had happened to her niece. This was not the same girl that had left them with August so happily on Friday morning. Lotti felt that Kathryn was not ready to talk. She took her hand, pressed it warmly and whispered, "I know, something happened to you. You can tell me when you are ready. I'll help you. I'll always be there for you."

Kathryn started crying and shook her head. Lotti didn't pry.

One more meal together was served at noon. At five in the afternoon, everyone boarded the cars and by dusk they arrived back at Blauenwald Castle.

CHAPTER 16

The Aftermath

Since Heidi had made up her mind to put the disturbing event concerning her daughter behind her as soon as possible—so their plans to stay in Europe for the rest of their vacation could go on as scheduled—she acted promptly after their return to Blauenwald. By herself she walked down to the village, entered the office of Dr. Amato and found *Fräulein* Frieda behind the desk.

"What can I do for you, Mrs. Carlton?" she asked politely.

Heidi felt terrified. Nobody, not even Kathryn, knew what she was up to. "I would like to make an appointment with the doctor," she said.

"For yourself?" asked Frieda.

"For my daughter."

"What seems to be the problem?"

"It's private." Heidi managed to say.

Frieda did not prod. "I understand. Would tomorrow afternoon at two o'clock be okay?"

"Yes. We'll be there."

"See you then, goodbye, Mrs. Carlton."

After Heidi had left, Frieda knocked on the Doctor's door. "Just made an appointment for you to see that American lady and her daughter tomorrow."

"Any idea what it's about?" Dr. Amato asked.

"Who knows? She said it's private."

"Aha, the daughter is about fifteen?"

"I think so."

"Interesting. Never a dull moment at that castle."

Heidi went up to the castle, deep in thoughts. What would Kathryn do? Well, what could she do? She was only fourteen. She would trust her, her mother. Wouldn't she? Maybe the whole thing was nothing. Maybe she wasn't pregnant. It was good that nobody knew. Well, tomorrow afternoon at least she and Kathryn would know.

Kathryn also had changed her mind. Like her mother, she wanted to know what was going on with her body. But she was not so sure she wanted to wait for weeks and pretend that nothing had happened. She wanted Jacob to know, whatever the result was. Therefore she agreed to go to Dr. Amato's office with her mother the next day.

The doctor and his assistant were ready for them at two o'clock. Kathryn was asked to undress and lie down on the cot in the little room adjoining the office. It took only a few minutes of administering a simple test and Dr. Amato was nodding his head.

"Sorry, my girl, I know you don't want to hear this …"

Kathryn stared at him, then at Frieda who held the test tube with a pink solution in her hand. "You mean, I am pregnant?"

Both nodded gravely. "Let's talk to your mother." The doctor said, "You may get dressed." He told Heidi the grim news. He couldn't refrain from asking, "Was it rape?"

Heidi didn't bother to answer this crude question. Her stern expression was answer enough for him.

"We can do a simple procedure and solve the problem." He was very sure of himself.

Slowly Kathryn put on her clothes and after a while Heidi came into the room.

"Kathryn, my dear, Dr. Amato tells me that it's a simple procedure to solve the problem. But you have to be willing to do this."

Kathryn was so stunned that she did not know what to say.

"We made an appointment for Friday to get this over with. It'll be the best we can do, Kathy!" She tried to embrace her daughter but was appalled by her stoic expression. Kathryn looked as though she was going to faint.

"The best thing we can do?" She repeated almost toneless.

She left the doctor's office on her mother's side, walking like a robot. The two days until Friday she stayed in her room not talking to anybody except her Aunt Lotti. Her mother brought her some food but she refused to eat. The others became concerned. Heidi told them that Kathryn had caught some bug and was sick.

On Thursday Kathryn and Lotti had a talk.

"Aunt Lotti, may I tell you something?"

"I told you that I'll help you to make a decision. I think I understand what's going on."

"Oh, Aunt Lotti, you and Mom are the only people who know. August raped me. I am pregnant and Mom wants me to have an abortion. Should I?"

Lotti thought for a while. "Kathy, I almost envy you. It happened on that bike ride around the lake, didn't it? You know, I always wanted a baby and for some reason I can't ever have one. And here are you, getting pregnant the first time you are with a boy, unfortunately the wrong one. But that precious seed is in you now. Any baby is a gift of God. Think hard before you destroy it. I repeat what I said before. I'll always help you. Please trust me." She hugged Kathryn. It was all that she could do. She held Kathryn in her arms. She whispered into her ear, "I'll help you with the baby." Kathryn nodded and responded to Lotti's hug.

"Thanks. Now I feel much better."

Lotti got up. Quietly she left the room.

Kathryn knew that it was up to her to decide. Both women, her mother and her aunt, wanted the best for her. *But what was the best?*

On Friday the girl and her mother went to the village and Dr. Amato and Frieda prepared Kathryn for the "procedure." Heidi was grateful that her daughter was so cooperative.

While Kathryn was lying on the cot, she was experiencing a moment of revelation. She saw her life enfolding in front of her. She knew that she loved Jacob. She wanted to spend her life with him. She wanted to tell him everything. She also knew that she had provoked August to rape her by flirting with him. During these few minutes the thoughtless girl became a sensitive woman. Her childhood had ended at the shore on Neusiedl Lake. No "procedure" by any doctor could fix her problem. She would fight them all. She would keep the baby.

When Frieda came into the room with the paraphernalia to prepare her for the abortion, her mind was made up. "Don't touch me," she told her sternly and no gentle persuasion of Frieda induced her to relent. When the doctor came in, Frieda shrugged her shoulders and said to him, "Guess she changed her mind."

"What's the matter, Miss, afraid I'll hurt you? It'll just take a second, come on; be a good girl."

"Leave me alone. I'll have the baby." Now it was Dr. Amato's turn to shrug his shoulders. Kathryn added, "And do not talk to anybody about all of this. Is this understood?" Resolutely she got up, shooed the baffled doctor and his assistant out of the room, got dressed, went out to her mother who now behaved like a robot, and together they left the office.

On the way home, Kathryn acted like her old self again. "You know, Mother, I am so happy that I made this decision. I will tell Jacob everything and he will understand. I could not live with all this secrecy. I am not too young to become a mother. I know this in my heart. Maybe August will feel sorry about this some day. But all that doesn't matter. Now I really have something to live for." Then she added: "But first Uncle Viktor and Aunt Betty have to know." (Kathryn always called them that and they liked it.)

Heidi was not so sure if she was ready for all this openness. But now many people would have to be told. How would they react to it? Little by little Heidi understood that this whole drama was a repetition of what had happened in 1975. Adele had chosen to keep her baby and Viktor had kept silent about it. The result was that the baby had been created, had grown up and had appeared at the castle, looking for his birth father who had not wanted him.

Kathryn had decided not to go that route. She knew from August's outburst at the lake that he did not want to acknowledge his baby. Though his reason to rape her was different from Viktor's—it boiled down to the same sad conclusion: a child not wanted by its own father. She accepted the new life in her womb and did not want its upbringing shrouded in secrecy. If Jacob rejected her now, so be it. She was considering the happiness of this baby. Maybe all the others would learn to see this "scandal" from a new, more human angle.

August stayed aloof and out of the way. He appeared only at meals.

Completely ignoring August, Kathryn had one-on-one conversations with Viktor and Betty and, finally, with Jacob. Both Viktor and Betty were shocked, but reacted differently. Viktor felt hurt by August (the reaction August had wanted to achieve), and sorry for Kathryn. Betty felt that Viktor's reputation—still fragile, though having improved over time—was at stake. If ever the fact became known that August had compromised an innocent girl, the people would say, "Like father like son" and blame Viktor for not bringing up his son the right way. Both begged Kathryn not to openly accuse August of having raped her. Kathryn assured both of them that this would never occur to her. After some deep contemplation she had come to the conclusion that she herself was to blame for encouraging August. Also Betty and Heidi talked to each other and the former learned that Dr. Amato probably knew that rape was involved. "He might put two and two together," warned Heidi. "He's smart."

Jacob had been wondering what was going on. He knew that ever since the trip to Newsiedl Lake something had changed with Kathryn. His great love for her gave him the strength to wait till she came to him. The departure of the Carltons was set for the following Monday and since it was already Saturday, he begged Kathryn to stay with him alone on Sunday. She readily agreed.

"I would have asked you the same thing, but you beat me to it."

She was happy to notice that his feelings for her were unchanged. If only he could understand what she had been going through and would agree with her decision to keep the baby!

Jacob and Kathryn walked through the yellowing vineyard and he started by pointing out the results of the lingering drought.

"Viktor is very concerned about the weather," he started, as if this was the problem Kathryn was wrestling with.

"I know; they might lose the harvest this year. But, Jacob, that's not what I want to talk about with you. We are leaving tomorrow and you of all people should know."

"Should know what? You have been moping around ever since that blasted bike ride with August. Why don't you tell me? Aren't you my girl anymore?

"More than ever, Jacob. I know now that I really love you. If it's not too late."

"What do you mean by that? Because you flirted with August?"

"It was more than that." Kathryn took a deep breath and her confession poured out of her like a gushing stream. "I know you were jealous. But I thought it would be fun to ride with August that day. In the beginning it was. But then he tricked me into having lunch at a place away from the trail. He raped me, Jacob. I had been dumb enough to trust him. It was something about getting back at Viktor because he had raped his mother. I couldn't do anything, He was so strong. I was only thinking of you, oh, Jacob, please believe me."

"So, what you are telling me, Kathy? You are pregnant now?"

"Yes, that's what I'm telling you. My mother wanted me to have an abortion but I couldn't do it." Then she added. "August doesn't want the baby. And I would never want to be married to him."

"I am glad about that." Jacob thought for a long while. Then he looked Kathryn straight into her eyes. "It's not the fact that you are pregnant," he said. "The point is that—even if you had not gotten pregnant—I won't be the first and only man in your life. Of course, it's hurting me. But all that's history now. We have to take it from here. Your honesty and you telling me that you still love me is all I want to hear. I believe you. I wish you would have come to me earlier, but it's not too late. August took advantage of your innocence just to get even with his miserable past. We'll ignore him. You and I will be together. And we'll raise this baby as ours."

"What do you mean?" asked Kathryn, still doubting Jacob's loyalty. "Do you still love me? Are we still going to be married, even if I have a baby by another man?"

"It's unfortunate that August did this to you, but, yes, I still love you. We are still getting married, maybe earlier than we had planned, and we'll have more babies together. If August doesn't want this baby—too bad for him."

It was gratifying for Jacob to observe Kathryn's face—so serious when she started her confession—change into glowing happiness. Jacob had his girl back, though everything had changed.

"Did you tell the others already? How many people know?"

"I told Viktor and Betty. They were shocked. Viktor is very disappointed in August. But now they understand why he wants to join the army."

Jacob thought to himself: *He's getting away with rape. He should go to jail. But I'll stay out of it.* He thought for a long time. Then he asked, "Who else knows?"

"Betty is going to tell my Grandma. I told Aunt Lotti and I think she told Uncle Peter. And, of course my Mom and Dad know. But that's just it; I don't want this to be a big secret. I want this baby to feel accepted and to be happy."

"And I will tell Nathan," said Jacob, nodding. "Unless he knows already from August. Those two have become pretty good friends. Now Viktor and I will have a man-to-man talk." He kissed Kathryn and went to Viktor's office.

Viktor was not surprised to see Jacob. Kathryn must have told him. That girl! She was full of surprises.

"Come in, Jacob, sit down, I think I know why you are here."

"Father," he said and Viktor felt a warm glow. "Kathryn told me that she had talked to you and Mom. It certainly was a shock to hear what happened, but I do love Kathryn and I still want to marry her. We will welcome this baby and raise it as our own."

"I like to hear that both of you accept the fact that your brother had to vent his unfortunate hatred against me in this way, without thinking of the consequences. What can I do for you?"

"I would like to marry Kathryn as soon as possible, so this baby has legitimate parents and does not feel abandoned. I realize that both of us are rather young and we need the help of our parents. Are you still thinking of letting me inherit the castle?"

Viktor felt ashamed. How much more mature was this young man than he had been at his age. Jacob, at only eighteen, was able to face the future. He would make a wonderful, responsible father. "Yes, Jacob, you shall be the owner of this castle. I could not think of a better person. It was a lucky day when I decided to marry your mother and adopt you two boys. Nathan has chosen to be a musician and you will learn everything that's necessary to become the future master of Blauenwald. August will now be fighting in Kosovo. He might want to start a military career. He told me this just yesterday, after Kathryn had informed me. He'll leave for Kosovo right after his twentieth birthday in the beginning of next year. Did you talk to Kathryn's parents already?"

"Not yet, but I do not anticipate any objection. I have always gotten along well with both of them. Father, we would like to get married around Christmas and then pursue our education. Kathryn will have the baby in California and her Aunt Lotti will help her during the first few years while Kathy is still in school. She'll graduate in Oakland and then join me here in Austria. That will be in four years. We talked about it this morning. I will start at the agricultural school in Graz and would appreciate your help with the tuition, room, and board. As soon as I graduate from that school in two years, I will spend all my time working with Paul and Sepp. Thanks to you and Mom I was able to graduate from high school and now I look forward to learning as much as I can in my chosen field. I do not need to go to Vienna. The agricultural college in Graz is plenty good enough for me. You know that going to school is not my favorite activity. I can hardly wait to be done with schooling and put my hands to work on real jobs."

Jacob took a deep breath; he never had given a speech that long.

"This sounds wonderful, Jacob. You'll have a nice wedding during the Christmas holidays and Kathryn will join our family. My son and my favorite niece!" (though this statement was not quite accurate, this was what he was feeling in his heart.)

"One more thing, Father," said Jacob, who felt very generous offering another item to make Viktor happy. "Could you and I go down to the record office and change my last name to 'Baumeister?' I know that you would like to keep up the family name.

Viktor's delighted face told enough. Jacob had made a solid hit.

So, a new generation was launched and four people who had considered themselves still "the younger ones" were going to become grandparents.

After the dust had settled and he had realized that he was not going to be punished for his serious crime, August had done sincere soul-searching. He realized that his misdeed had affected several people who had not done him any harm. The one person whom he had intended to hurt, Viktor, seemed rather happy with the outcome of the events. No one was going to sue him in court. No one was hindering him leaving for war, either. No one seemed to really want him to stay, except Liesl. He began to doubt the importance of being alive. Maybe he could become an excellent soldier and start a brand-new life. If only …! If only he could erase what he had done. He felt the least tiny budding of remorse.

By evening every living soul in the castle and in the village had heard the news. The absolute truth did not have to be broadcast. This is what people would say: The young couple had gotten intimate a little too early. Therefore there would be a wedding a few months before the first baby made its appearance. Happens all the time! And the young bride would like to stay at her own home in America for a few years while her young husband was getting his education. All of Blauenwald would understand. It was what people would talk about.

If only Dr. Amato wouldn't leak the real truth.

That this would not happen, Betty—having heard from Heidi that Dr. Amato knew it was rape and was shrewd enough to figure out the truth—decided to scare the ambitious doctor. She went down to his office, talked to him in his private office, and assured him she would send a letter to every villager about boycotting his services. Another doctor would be encouraged to establish office in Blauenwald and he and *Fräulein* Frieda would have to leave town. The castle people had that much clout in the community.

This helped. Not a word was leaked about the rape and who the perpetrator was. Somehow Dr. Amato had found out that August was the real father of Kathryn's baby but he managed to keep it to himself. Not even Frieda heard about it.

On Monday morning Viktor brought the five Carltons to Leibnitz from where the bus delivered them to Graz to the train for Munich. They spent ten days with their relatives in Bergen. Peter flew home to his family in California.

After summer vacation ended, Nathan and Jacob left for their respective colleges.

CHAPTER 17

Reminiscence

In the year 1996, roughly a year after the big reunion and twenty-one years after Viktor had confided to the priest that he had sired a child against his wishes during a state of being under the influence of alcohol, the Baumeisters sat together with their extended family on the shady verandah at the southwest corner on the second floor of Blauenwald Castle. The small group of people consisted of Viktor, his wife Betty, their young daughter Liesl, Betty's mother Marie Fromm, as she was called in Austria, twenty-one-year old Nathan and his almost nineteen-year-old brother Jacob. It was late afternoon after a scorching hot day in April and the tall spruce on the corner of the verandah spent welcome shade from the slanting sunrays. It was an unusual hot spring and the weatherman did not predict precipitation in the near future. After some welcomed downpours in February, the grapes had started to set, but needed more rain badly.

August had enlisted as a volunteer in the Serbian Army; nobody except the close family knew why. He had left right after his twentieth birthday in February of '96.

Manfred Sattler, their good friend and neighbor, had just joined the group to take a little rest from the daily work on his estate. He had ridden over from Reichenfels, had left his horse at the Baumeisters' stable, and was heartily welcomed by the Blauenwald people. They were enjoying the lovely view over the rolling hills of southern Styria, now predominantly parched yellowish because of the persisting drought. So far it had been a very bad year for the winegrowers in this southern part of Austria. The drought had hit the estate of Castle Blauenwald just as bad as the other areas in Styria. But, unlike the other *Weingüter*, Blauenwald featured a variety of crops, like hay, corn, carrots, and beans, not as susceptible to the drought as grapevines.

The men were engulfed in serious talk. Betty's two sons had come home from their respective schools, Nathan from the Music Academy of Vienna, Jacob from the agricultural college in Graz. Young Liesl sat close to her mother, not losing a word of the conversation.

After first discussing the close-by war in Bosnia, which had ended abruptly when NATO air squadrons bombed the area and caused considerable loss of life and destruction of property, the conversation turned to the perpetrator of this air attack, the Americans. The neutral Austrians had a critical view of Americans and their president, Bill Clinton, who had been instrumental in sending the NATO troops. Manfred turned to his friend.

"No offence, Viktor, but do you, obviously a peace-loving man, approve of the American president's decision to bomb civilians and innocent children?"

Viktor, who was appreciating the chance to air his opinion in front of family and friends, feeling strongly for his country's neighbors, but also wishing to defend actions of the Americans, answered, "I'm not a politician, Manfred. But though I don't agree with using brutal force, I think that one thing has been a good outcome: the war in Bosnia is over. Our sons would have to go to war in Bosnia if this war had dragged out into the future." He was referring to the possibility that Austria might join the peacekeeping troops that were sent to Bosnia to maintain order in the newly formed areas of Bosnia and Herzegovina.

"Granted," intervened Manfred, "but a new war is brewing. Albanian rebels in Kosovo are killing thousands of Serbs because they don't like the outcome of the war."

Betty joined in the conversation. "Our August is now fighting with the Serbs against the Albanians. He wrote last week that the Kosovo Liberation Army is giving them a hard time. He hates those Albanians because they were instrumental in killing his mother. He cannot forget what those Muslims did to his people."

The men looked concerned. "What a shame. Such a promising young man."

Now Liesl spoke up, "Why did August have to go away? I didn't want him to go!"

Mary Fromm declared, "I don't either, Liesl. Why do you men always have to talk about politics? If all this talk about a new war isn't bad enough, what about the drought this year?"

Manfred sighed deeply. "Oh yes, the drought." After a pregnant pause he stated, "The country needs rain badly. Last time it rained was end of February. The weatherman has no good news for us."

"The drought hits all of us," agreed Viktor.

Manfred was considering that Viktor's estate only has a small, but very exclusive grape: the Muscat. It was more like a hobby, but nevertheless—the vineyard planted by Viktor's parents was essential for bringing in revenues to pay for the upkeep of the castle. Manfred's estate, on the other hand, was one of the large wine producing enterprises; he now had three quarters of his 20,000 acres of arable land planted in grapes and had a staff of fifty workers depending on him. His large wine processing facilities made his estate the center for the surrounding wine growers.

While these talks were going on, the housekeeper, *Fräulein* Hanni, having replaced *Frau* Grete Schwarz who lately was riddled with arthritis and could not work anymore, had poured more red wine into the glasses in front of the men. The women tended to their sewing and knitting. The air was heavy with the oppressing heat.

Viktor nodded his head toward Manfred. "My beautiful Muscats won't fruit in this drought. If there is no rain this summer, we won't have grapes to harvest in September."

"Time to pray," offered Mary now instead of her late husband trying to solve problems with religion. She pondered, "We had to survive several of those droughts in California. Of course, we did not grow grapes, but many a grape grower had to suffer great losses when their vineyards were scorched. Somehow our Lord helped them to survive."

Betty looked at her mother and smiled. "I love you, Mom," she told her. "Without you I would have never made it here."

She addressed her husband, "Aren't you glad, Viktor, that we have Mother living here at the castle, so at least one of the older generation is still with us?"

"Yes, of course, my dear." Then his face became grave.

"Betty, we went through hard times together, but this time I am afraid we won't even make enough money to pay our taxes."

Betty's expression of sympathy broadened into a smile. She half-closed her eyes and carried her thoughts back. "I am so glad that we had that wonderful reunion last year while things were still going well here at Blauenwald. To see all our old friends from California again and to show them around in our beautiful country. To see all those pictures of Springlake! And to hear them tell us about how that little town has developed. They even have a library now! I guess our storytelling circle has helped a great deal with that. I wish we could have a library in Blauenwald. I could work there as a librarian."

Then she added, "And I am also happy that you could afford the trip to California in 1991." She smiled and looked at her husband.

Viktor emptied the glass in front of him. Betty looked up. She was still worried about Viktor's drinking and silently motioned to Hanni not to fill his glass again. Viktor smiled at his wife. He knew that she was concerned about his drinking and he wished she would join him. But she—a nondrinker—could not change long-time habits. She'd rather change her husband's habit of sipping too much alcohol. She was still the old Betty who preferred to be dressed in simple, somber clothes, having her hair put up in a bun, and not using any make-up. She was the quiet, steady force in his life and he could not live without her.

Viktor turned to Manfred and said, "I was barely able to pay my taxes at the beginning of this year and even had to postpone sorely needed reparations in our castle. If there is no harvest, we'll have to borrow money."

"It's the same with me," replied Manfred. "But it's different with you. You have other crops, Viktor. Maybe your pumpkin fields and the winter wheat will resist the drought better than my grapes. Anyway, you are not solely dependent on your vineyards as I am. Do you remember the drought years of the early 1980s when you were so occupied with taking over the estate after the loss of your parents? At that time some people had the brilliant idea of tainting cheap wine with glycol to enhance the taste and strike it rich. This almost crushed Austria's reputation as one of the leading wine producers all over the world."

"Of course I remember all about the scandal. How could I forget? That's when our Sepp got into trouble. Yes, it was happening at the time when I took over the estate. I was so busy then with learning to be the master and I still trusted Sepp completely. Only after I brought Betty home and relaxed a little did I learn what had happened. The whole thing became public and one of the culprits leaked to the court that Sepp had a hand in this and was convicted to serve four years in jail. Then all hell broke loose and I was by myself—responsible not only for a large estate, but also for a large family. That's when you offered to ask Paul to help me."

"It was good for both of you," said Manfred. "Paul—at that time—did not have a clear direction what to do with his life. He was mooning after Gerda who was then in love with that priest. Those four years of working for you have made a man out of Paul. So that's when you actually found out about that disaster?"

"Right, and as you can imagine, I was shocked. Paul was great, but he did not have the experience Sepp had. When the four years were over, Sepp had "model inmate status" and was released. He admitted his guilt to me and promised not to join any questionable schemes in the future. I forgave him for working behind my back and reinstated him as my manager. For a while he assisted Paul, and now both are working together."

Manfred asked, "What does Paul say? And have you talked to Sepp lately?"

Viktor debated Manfred's question in his mind for a while. Then he said, "Sepp thinks that we should invest in a sprinkler system. He already wanted my parents to do that in the 1970s. My parents never had to endure years without rain, so the problem did not come up while they were in charge. They did not want to spend the money for installing a sprinkler system."

"I can't blame them," said Manfred. "It costs quite a bit and what if there is no water to sprinkle with?"

Viktor sighed and replied, "I would do it if I had the money. Just to insure for the future. Of course, it's too late for this year. And, you are right. How much good does such a system do if there is no water around to sprinkle with?"

"It would involve digging deeper wells."

Then Manfred asked, "Any news from California, Jacob?"

"Kathryn and little Karl are doing great. Lotti also wrote. The baby has gained ten pounds and weighs now close to twenty pounds. He was a heavy baby to begin with, about nine and a half pounds. Nearly doubled his weight during those first three months."

"Twenty pounds!" exclaimed Viktor who was thinking in European pounds. "Liesl wasn't even twenty pounds when she was two years old."

"That's normal," said practical Jacob. He turned to Viktor. "You must consider that pounds in America are less than in Austria. And also, Karl is a boy, Liesl a girl."

Manfred smiled at Jacob. "You sound like a good dad. Really proud of your first one!"

Then Mary spoke. "Let's be grateful for all the good things that happened in the past: the wonderful reunion, having all family and friends together, the wedding of Jacob and Kathryn, the birth of little Karl, and all of us healthy. A lot to thank for. Now we just have to worry that our August will do all right in Kosovo.

"Amen," said Nathanial, who had just joined the group.

The gong sounded. It was time to get ready for the evening meal.

CHAPTER 18

Closure

After his twentieth birthday August had left for Kosovo. After one letter in May the Baumeisters did not hear from him again. In the beginning of July a letter arrived from the major in charge of the troops in Kosovo. *Something's happened to August* was Viktor's first thought and he was right. The major informed Viktor of a bloody attack of the KLA and that August Boraq, son of Viktor Baumeister at Blauenwald, Styria, was severely wounded and needed to be transported to a stationary hospital.

> *...We are overwhelmed with wounded soldiers and do not have the facilities to take proper care of your son. We are now stationed near Pristina. Please arrange for transporting Private Boraq to Austria as soon as possible.*
>
> *Sincerely, Major Winfried Frank, July 5, 1996.*

Viktor and Jacob left the same evening for Pristina. They made their way through a chaotic field set-up. Weary soldiers dressed in fatigues were swarming around. August was delirious when they arrived at the primitive tent outside the war scene, where they had laid the wounded soldier. His shrapnel wound in the right thigh had been infected and the army surgeon had to amputate his leg. Carefully they carried the sick boy to the station wagon, made him comfortable as well as they could and several hours later had him installed in his old room at the castle, prepared by *Fräulein* Hanni. Betty and Gerda took care of him around the clock and Dr. Amato came up daily to inspect the slowly healing wound. Liesl sat at his bedside, holding his hand, whenever she could between school time and chores. She helped him eat the food that *Fräulein* Hanni had prepared. Everyone in the castle was amazed at the dedication and persistence the young girl revealed.

Two weeks after August had come home he only showed little improvement. One morning after waking up he saw his sister sitting by his bedside, looking at him sorrowfully.

"Liesl," he said, "could you do me a favor?"

"Anything, dear. What is it?"

"Could you bring Nathanial to talk to me?"

"Certainly." Liesl got up and checked Nathanial's room. The priest had already left. She hoped to find him at the church. He was in his office preparing the sermon for next Sunday. He motioned the girl to sit down and asked if he could help her. Liesl's agitated demeanor told him that something was very wrong.

"Father," she said, "August is doing poorly this morning. He wants to see you. Could you possibly come with me? I think it's urgent."

Nathanial grabbed his Bible and followed her. He found the boy writhing in pain. Liesl left the two alone. The priest took August's hand and pressed it warmly.

"You wanted to talk to me, August?"

"Father." August pleaded. "I don't want to live anymore. My life is useless. The world is better off without me. Please help me find peace."

"August," the priest said sternly, "aren't you a good Catholic? Don't even consider taking your own life. God gave you this precious gift. You will get better and still have a meaningful life ahead of you. You are surrounded by people who love you."

"It's too late, Father." He observed the sad look on Nathanial's face and decided to pretend a change of mind. Nathanial would never support a mortal sin. Suicide, he knew, was a carnal sin. *Would Raphael have understood?* "I'll try," he whispered. "Please let Dr. Amato come up and talk to me."

Nathanial did not know much about the Japanese doctor. He understood that August wanted medical advice. He kissed August's forehead and told him, "That's right, my friend. Have the doctor help you to overcome these dark thoughts. I shall pray for you."

August feigned sleep and the priest left quietly. He told the concerned parents to have the doctor come up to the castle. Dr. Amato and August had a private consultation.

When August could sit up and had enough strength to hold a pen in his hand, he asked Liesl for writing utensils and, after she had left him for the night, wrote the following letter.

> *Dear People at the Castle,*
>
> *I don't want to live like this. I have been with you for almost ten years. You all have been good to me. I know I made it hard for some of you, especially for you, Father, I know I was wrong taking out my bad feelings on you. You really tried hard to make good for abandoning me earlier. I forgive you now and hope you forgive me for being an ungrateful son.*
>
> *Kathryn, will you ever forgive me?*
>
> *Jacob, I wish you and Kathryn will lead a happy life.*
>
> *Father, please bury me as August Boraq Baumeister.*
>
> *That's all. Goodbye. I'll go back to be with my mother.*
>
> *August.*

They found the young man the next morning, the letter still in his hand, an empty bottle of pain killers next to him. Who had given him the pills? Most likely Dr. Amato who had visited August every day. Liesl was inconsolable. She had been August's closest confidant and could not believe that this had happened. Viktor took the letter and read it to the others. Everyone felt that August had died peacefully and without malicious feelings against anyone. Betty pressed Viktor's hand and looked at him lovingly. She felt that her husband now had finally found peace of mind and was able to leave the past behind him.

Dark clouds had been gathering on the horizon.

After the funeral service the congregation of the little church left slowly. The black-shrouded casket with August's body was carried by the pall bearers to the hill that contained the burial vault for the Baumeister family. There had been a discussion among the immediate family members where to put August's remains. It was clear that because of the manner of his death he could not be put into the ancestral vault, but was given his own place on a small plot next to the vault. He had taken his own life and according to church principles should not be buried with people who had died the ordinary way. His spirit was now united again with his beloved mother's and there was closure for everyone. The Brenners and the Carltons had sent wreaths and the Baumeisters and their extended family and friends accompanied August to his last resting place where the successor of Raphael officiated the funereal rites. Nathanial told the assembled mourners about God's will that had led the restless young man back to his place of origin and had allowed his soul to stay with his ancestors. No mention was made of the empty pill bottle—there was no need. After the grave diggers had added the finishing touches to the burial pit, the pall bearers carried the coffin to the gravesite, lowered it into the ground, and the assembled people threw handfuls of earth onto the lid. Workers finished the job by shoveling dirt from a prepared pile nearby. Nathan played Jules Massenet's haunting song *Meditation* on his violin and after the last sounds still vibrated the mourners left the grave slowly, walked the path to the linden alley and the villagers turned to the right, going home to their houses, while the castle people turned left and passed the castle gate. Here they separated, the staff gathered at the dining hall on the ground floor where Gerda and Hanni had prepared the festive meal for the staff. The family and invited friends mounted the stairs to the formal dining room. Viktor had asked Grete, who was too old to be part of the procession, to supervise the preparations for the funeral meal in the dining room.

During the funeral proceedings, the entire sky had turned dark with heavy rain clouds. After the last sounds of Massenet's music faded away, the first lightning rays flashed across the sky and thunder followed. The first rain drops fell and by the time everyone was back at the castle and their homes, the entire area was engulfed in solid rain fall. The people, drenched but happy, thanked God for the needed rain. The parched earth received the welcome downpour. Everyone was relieved. It rained for several days.

"So, finally we got our prayers answered. Hope it's not too late," said Viktor, heaving relief.

EPILOGUE

Beyond 1996

The castle returned to its tranquil state. The thunder storm in 1996 had saved the crop. Viktor and Betty were now the old ones and they retired from being owners and made room for the young Baumeisters. They were by themselves again. People had learned to like and respect them. Often they saw them walking through the village hand in hand, followed by a descendent of old Peter, the faithful shepherd. After Mary's death in the last year of the twentieth century, they moved to the Fromms' apartment. They also traveled. They kept up their relationship with their American friends and relatives, and they all visited each other from time to time.

Jacob and Kathryn had finished their education and were now the new, young, and energetic owners. Together with Paul and Gerda they managed the buildings and lands of Blauenwald Castle. After the master suite on the second floor became available, they moved in. Their son Karl developed into a sturdy youngster who loved his new castle home. Lotti's gentle care had started him off right. Other children were born.

Fortunately none of them inherited the fateful genes of the Carlton family that had resulted in a handicapped child. But love and excellent care had made it possible for Hansi to lead a comfortable, though sheltered, life. He could take advantage of the quickly developing Independent Living organizations. He kept up his sunny outlook on life. He even was able to make some money working as a clerk at a local shop in California.

Liesl had decided to become a leader of young people and also to pursue a religious career. She was well on the way to achieving both goals. She graduated with high honors in her chosen field of education from the Catholic college sponsored by the *Herz-Jesu-*

Kirche in Graz. She was the youngest student when she entered the Catholic community at this church, took her first vows, and changed from being a novice to becoming a teaching sister. After several years of work outside she took her final vows and became a nun. She still continued to teach. She was a wonderful educator and was loved by all her students. She never forgot her half-brother August. Whenever her busy schedule allowed it, she brought flowers to the little graveside next to the family vault and had intimate conversations with her beloved kin. An attractive grave stone read:

Here rests August Boraq Baumeister,
son of Viktor Baumeister and Adele Boraq,
born 1976, died 1996.
May he find eternal peace.

It was Liesl who took care of the plot and kept it free of weeds. Often she sat on the little bench that her father had made for her, beheld the gravestone lovingly, and cried bitter tears. August was the love of her life.

Sepp retired from being the assistant manager at the castle when he turned fifty-five. He settled in Blauenwald Village, running a small store selling and repairing farming equipment. Viktor had managed to persuade the banker Hermann Reich to grant him a loan to open his business. Sepp was successful in this endeavor and could live comfortably from what his store provided. In only two years he was able to pay back his loan from the bank. He became a respected citizen of Blauenwald and was often seen at the Buschenschank drinking his well-earned beer and talking with other citizens.

Dr. Amato and Frieda decided to get married and, due to their ever growing practice, were able to purchase a home large enough to accommodate his parents who had been living in a small apartment in Graz and were overjoyed to be close to their son and his family.

Raphael pursued his high goals and became archbishop in due time.

Blauenwald Castle was prepared to stay on Castle Hill for many years to come, to see generations come and go, to watch scandals evolve and subside, and to endure catastrophes, natural as well as man-made ones. People in Blauenwald Village continued to look up to the castle as their fondest possession and to the owners as their leaders.

List of Characters

In order of appearance in the text
The number in parenthesis indicates date of birth

Raphael Garibaldi, (1946) Young ordained priest who takes over the parish of Blauenwald

Gerda Wanz, (1949) Housekeeper at the castle

Viktor Baumeister, (1947) Future owner of the castle

Alfred Baumeister, (1906) Son of previous owner, Rudolf Baumeister, and Friederike von Ebersbach

Rudolf Baumeister, (1880) original owner, father of Alfred, later also of Karl

Maria Baumeister, (1884) Rudolf's mistress, later his wife

Friederike von Ebersbach, (1872) Rudolf's first wife

Karl Baumeister, (1914) Son of Rudolf and Maria, half-brother of Alfred

Susanne Baumeister, born Fischer, (1913) Alfred's wife

Margarete (Grete) Schwarz, (1901) Housekeeper at the castle before Gerda, later cook, oldest person alive at the castle

Fritz Schwarz, (1900) her husband

Manfred Sattler, (1914) neighbor wine producer, friend of Baumeisters

Josef (Sepp) Wanz, (1946) Manager of Blauenwald estate, brother of Gerda

Adele Boraq, (1961) Gypsy girl, mother of Viktor's child, August

Paul Sattler, (1951) Manfred's son, in love with Gerda Wanz

Ursula Sattler, (1919) Manfred's wife, Paul's mother, dies 1973

Erma Brenner, born Fischer, (1925) Lake Dweller*, American from Germany, first cousin of Susanne Fisher, married Hans Brenner in 1953, lives in Oakland, California with her family

Berta, (1946) Sepp's helper and girlfriend, daughter of washerwoman, lives in Blauenwald Village

Hans Brenner, (1921) Lake Dweller*, Erma Brenner's husband, also of German descent.

Heidi Carlton, born Brenner, (1955) Oldest daughter of Hans and Erma Brenner, wife of Richard Carlton, lives in Oakland, California

Lotti Updike, born Brenner, (1960) Second daughter, Heidi's younger sister, wife of George Updike, becomes Lake Dweller*

Peter Brenner, (1967) Son of Hans and Erma

Betty Goldstein Baumeister, born Fromm, (1948) Wife of Viktor Baumeister, was married to David Goldstein

Mary (Marie) Fromm, (1921) Wife of Luther Fromm, Betty's mother, from Germany, Lake Dweller*

Luther Fromm, (1919) Originally from Germany, moved to America after the war;.he and Mary are former Lake Dwellers*, moved to the castle in Austria in 1985

Nathan Goldstein, (1975) Older son of Betty and David Goldstein

Jacob Goldstein, (1978) Nathan's younger brother

David Goldstein, (1949) Betty's former husband, father of Nathan and Jacob, died in the late 1970s

Hermann Reich, Banker in Blauenwald

Gottlieb Hausmann, Mayor of Blauenwald

Hanni, (1971) Young helper at the castle

Erika, (1971) Young helper at the castle

Dr. Amato, (1945) Medical Doctor in Blauenwald, from Japan

Dr. Richter, Attorney in Graz

Dr. Hollman, Medical Doctor in Blauenwald before Dr. Amato

Frieda, Dr. Amato's assistant and lover

Liesl Baumeister, (1986) Daughter of Viktor and Betty Baumeister

August Boraq, (1976) Illegitimate son of Viktor and Adele

Kathryn Carlton, (1981) Older daughter of Richard and Heidi Carlton

Richard Carlton, (1953) Heidi's husband, teacher of the Handicapped

Gretchen Carlton, (1986) Younger sister of Kathryn

Luise Gilmann, (1965) Neighbor of the Brenners in Oakland, California

Anna Gilmann, (1908) Luise's grandmother

Rupert, (1916) Gate keeper at Blauenwald Castle

Nathaniel, (1952) Priest replacing Raphael

Fay and Bob Foster, (1930, 1926) Lake Dwellers*, start the storytelling circle together with the Brenners

Jean Dubois, (1928) Lake Dweller* Rich oilman from Texas

Ellen Dubois, born McGregor, (1929) His wife, Lake Dweller*

Jeannie Dubois, (1962) Daughter of Jean and Ellen Dubois, actress

Hansi Carlton, (1988) Third child of Richard and Heidi Carlton, slightly autistic

Arnold Schwarzenegger, (1947) Famous film star in the 1980s and 1990s

Gordon Newman, (1941) Journalist from Rivertown, Lake Dweller*, used to own a tiny cabin at Springlake

Lily Carpenter Newman, born Silverman, (1954) Wife of Gordon Newman, daughter of former Lake Dweller*, Esther Silverman, divorced from first husband, Walter Carpenter

Lexy and Carly Newman, (1986) Twin daughters of Gordon and Lily Newman

George Updike, (1959) Lotti Updike's husband, Lake Dweller*

Dr. Lee and Gisela Warner, (1933 and 1934) Former Lake Dwellers*, both teachers at Berkeley University

Young Karl, (1996) Son of August and Kathryn, raised by Jacob and Kathryn

* The term "Lake Dweller" refers to Schmidt's earlier book *The Lake Dwellers* (2007).

Explanation of German Expressions

Abendbrot: evening meal
Aufgeräumt: put in order
Aufschnitt: cold cuts
Bank: bank
Bierstein: mug for beer
Blutwurst: blood sausage
Buschenschank: tavern
Dr.: abbreviation for *"Doktor,"* in German speaking countries used
  as title not only for medical doctors. Dr. Richter would be listed
  as *Dr. jur. Richter*—as an attorney he studied law. Dr. Amato's
  title would be *Dr. med.*
Amato. Donauturm: a landmark on the shore of the Danube in
  Vienna (similar to the space needle in Seattle, Washington)
Frau: means "Mrs." and also "woman"
Frühstück: breakfast
Gnädige Frau: Honored Lady, a term used by lower class people
  addressing higher class people.
Gymnasium: high school
Herr: means "Mr." and also "gentleman" In European countries
  Herr und *Frau* is used together with titles in salutations.
  Example: *Frau Dr. Hollmann, Herr Dr. Richter. An "n"* after
  Herr denotes the accusative case.
Heuriger: house wine from this year
Hofburg: palace housing various attractions for visitors, also still
  residence for royalty
Imbiß: ʃnack
Jause: in-between meal, often cookies, light sandwiches, milk,
  juice, etc.
Kernöl: oil pressed from sunflower seeds
Knödel: dumplings with various fillings

Kristkindel: Austrian "Santa" brings presents; a beautiful girl angel

Leberwurst: liver sausage

Lederhosen: leather pants

Lieder: songs

Marktplatz: market place

Meißen: very expensive China made in the city of Meißen, Germany

Mittagessen: lunch, big meal of the day

Nationalbibliothek: National Library

Opernhaus: opera house

Österreich: Austria

Ostmark: Austria when it was a German province during the Hitler years

Pension: bed and breakfast inns, sometimes on farms

Prunksaal: grand hall

Ringstraße: main avenue in Vienna, skirting the inner city

Rittersaal: hall of the warriors

Sacher Torte: special tart, made only at the Sacher Café in Vienna

Schatzkammer: Treasury

Schwarzbrot: dark bread made from unprocessed flower, like pumpernickel

Schwarzer Peter: card game like old made, but the single card is a male cat

Seewinkel: Southern part of the land surrounding Neusiedl Lake

Semmeln: buns

Shabbat: Sabath, Jewish weekend

Spuk: inexplicable noise in the attic; pronounced like "spook"

Ungarn: Hungary

Volksoper: opera house for the people

Weingut: wine producing estate

Wiener Schnitzel: thin slices of veal, coated with breadcrumbs and pan-fried.

Wiener Staatsoper: Vienna State Opera

Willkommen: welcome

Zauberflöte: Magic Flute, opera by Mozart

Zwetschgenknödel: dumplings filled with prunes